PRAISE

"Jaskowski wields words like weapons, his prose quick and sharp as a butterfly knife. The result: a truly original work in the corpus of body horror."

— BRENDAN VIDITO, *PORNOGRAPHY FOR THE END OF THE WORLD, NIGHTMARES IN ECSTASY*

MUTANT CIRCUIT

MARK JASKOWSKI

Dedicated to David Cronenberg and Victor Serge.
If we survive this winter, we will have become something
new and beautiful and terrible.

CONTENTS

One   1

Two   23

Three   47

Four   57

Five   77

Six   97

Seven   119

Eight   139

Later   173

Acknowledgments   177

About the Author   179

Also from Weirdpunk Books   181

ONE

THREE DAYS AFTER THEY DELIVER THE MEDICAL
supplies, liberated from a Miami pharmacy unlikely to
report the theft, the customer rings Anja's cell, exactly the
way she'd told him not to.

"We ought to be using burners," Cortland says, and he's
right, but it's never been enough of an issue to necessitate
the hassle.

The customer's cryptic. Careful. He won't talk specifics
on the phone, only a large-ish number that he doesn't call
dollars, so Anja agrees to meet him behind the strip mall.

Anja and Cortland pull out of the motel parking lot,
bags already loaded in the back seat. Cortland turns them
away from the interstate they'd planned on and aims back
into the populated part of town. A couple gas stations and
then some fenced neighborhoods, then a strip of big-box
stores, and Palm Gulf springs into street light.

They drive north to a ragged strip mall tucked into an
intersection between mid- and downtown, a pocket of
commercial zoning largely cut off from student and townie

cash flows. Parking lot in front, a few spaces around back. Anja pulls in back.

The buyer is not waiting for them. Anja waves for Cortland to cut the lights. "But keep it running."

"I can drive," Cortland says.

"You keep saying that."

"Last time wasn't my fault," through his teeth. "You know damn well—"

Anja waves it off, shouldn't have said anything. The money the buyer handed over for the needles was real enough that she's willing to give him a couple minutes, but she's not so relaxed that she's willing to risk Cortland's flaring ego, burning bright around its wounded spot.

The location makes her skin crawl. It's quiet but still too well-lit, too many roads nearby. She opens her mouth to tell Cortland to haul ass, to take what they've been paid so far and head toward the beach, maybe see some of Florida that isn't all mud and scratchy grass and that creepy gray moss. One of the doors opens in the back of the strip mall, cuts a weak shadow into the ambient street light.

"What a respectable fellow," Cortland says. "He's got himself a storefront."

"Just remember which door."

Cortland would anyway.

The buyer doesn't approach the car. Waits for Anja to get out and then frowns like she's not moving fast enough. She eases the door not all the way closed and approaches him.

"I need something done," he says.

"Well?"

The man looks down the road, describes a woman and a truck. Gives them a plate number and ten percent up front.

Anja wants to argue the percentage but it's already almost as much as they made from what they came to town for.

Anja shrugs her way back into the car. Maybe the woman won't have made much of her head start.

They drive until they see taillights and Cortland cuts the lights.

KATHERINE'S TORN the stitches out of her side and now her blood's pooling in the folds of her tee shirt, pattering onto the center console. She wrenches the truck's wheel to the right, off the road. Dull white flash of pain. The pattering speeds up. A warm trickle creeps down her arm, then slows again when she straightens the wheel. The truck jams over a rut, and blood flicks off her fingertip onto the windshield.

Like it wasn't already hard enough to see.

She can't quite remember. Can't quite remember how much she can't remember, but she awoke in some storage room covered in sheets of plastic and something pressing against her skin from inside. She didn't notice the stitches until she'd already clawed them out. There were footsteps in the other room, and she crashed out the heavy steel back door. The truck, she found unlocked out back of some bar two buildings away. Revolver in the glovebox.

Red reflectors fade behind her with the road. Katherine keeps the headlights off and her foot off the brake, but now the tall sugarcane is coming up way too fast and she has to stomp her foot down on that spongy left pedal, even keep it there for a couple seconds. Suspension jouncing slower and slower.

In the red wash her brake lights make of the field between the truck and the road, in the instant before she cuts them, a pair of headlights flicks to life. Obnoxious blue-white xenon, drowning the sugarcane in front of her in shadow, the field in glare. Katherine steps back on the accelerator, to ease forward through the stalks, push through hard enough to keep course, but she gives it too much gas. The rear wheels skitter over dirt, skid hard to the side.

Gravity comes up, surges from below Katherine. The sugarcane twists up and around in front of her, just a few yard out of reach, and then it's all airbags and shattering glass.

THE TRUCK DISAPPEARS from the road in front of them, and could wait until they're passed and slip away, now, but the woman blasts those brake lights like a signal flare, turns Cortland and Anja into red silhouettes. Anja breaths out, fast. It was close.

Cortland hitches the car off the road and draws them up to the truck, just a few yards shy of the sugarcane. The driver-side door's on top now, flapping open. Long bloody smear along the running board, then down to the woman slumped in the dirt.

Cortland snorts. "Doesn't run so damn fast now, does she."

Anja doesn't say anything, but does step out of the car first so that, approaching the woman, she's in front. The woman rears up around the wound seeping through her fingers. Tiny glinting revolver in her other hand. Pop and flash and the air next to Anja's leg moves. Anja shoves her boot heel forward, gets a dull smack from the woman's chin. The gun drops to the dirt.

Behind her, Cortland curses. She looks back, sees him upright but clutching his thigh in both hands, mouth gaping in the shadows of his face.

She gets the woman's gun and looks for a heartbeat. Finds instead a dull throb in the woman's skin. Less a pulse than a crawling. The woman doesn't move.

Anja hauls the woman up by her armpits and drags until she can shove her into the passenger seat. Her head catches the edge of the roof. New trickle of blood, the least of her problems. She sprawls over toward the driver's side. Wet squish of the gash in her side on the gearshift, bubbling of too-solid blood around the knob. Anja swallows hard, waits, but the woman doesn't move. Anja nods and slams the door.

Cortland's still standing, and she'll give him credit for it, but he's not doing much else besides clutching the bullet hole in his leg.

"You're not dying. It missed the important shit."

"And you know that? How do you know that?"

Anja shrugs. "You're still standing." She cracks open the chamber of the revolver and shows him. "It's a fucking popgun, Cortland. People have been shot with these breaking into houses and not noticed until they got home."

"Like hell. Like hell they have."

She braces her arm under him and crutches him to the back of the station wagon. "I'm sorry about this." Pulls open the back hatch.

Cortland groans about it, how there aren't any seats in

the back, how the bleeding woman's in the passenger seat, but he crawls in, curls around his shot leg.

Anja closes the hatch and looks back at the truck. Normally she'd prefer to torch the thing, use the two cans of gasoline they're carting around for exactly that purpose, but it's a client kind of deal and the client said not to bother, that their prisoner's DNA wouldn't get anybody anywhere, that the fire would call attention faster than an abandoned truck.

She shrugs, gets in the car. Creaking vinyl, cracked plastic, and something else now, too. A rich sweet rotting smell, like blue-black skin sluicing over fat gone green. Maggot country. Anja stares at the woman. She doesn't *look* rotting. Anja holds her breath and peels the woman off the gearshift. Slurping skin and hot rush of that sickly smell, and the wound on the woman's side is bigger than Anja thought.

The woman's still breathing, though. Anja can't decide if that's a good thing. She rolls down the window and hangs her head out for fresher air and bounces them back to the road, toward the dumpster behind a closed-down store Butler chose for their drop-off point.

AN HOUR AND A HALF LATER, the wind sighs through the railings of the third-floor balcony outside so it sounds like waves cresting over soft sand, and for a moment Butler isn't up to his elbows in Katherine's stomach. Isn't going to have to scrape *that* out from under his fingernails later.

But then the gap between this gust and the next one

stretches just longer enough that he slips through it and the salt air fades from his mental skin. The hotel phases back in around him, green couch and thin burgundy carpet. Chlorine from the pool mingling with mildew in the air, sharp and soft. Iron tang on the back end of that cocktail, blood misting up to flavor the air.

On the plastic sheet wrapped around the bed, Katherine's eyes are wide, still. Veins straining in a way that gives the illusion of motion.

Her face is frozen, though, in a chemical rictus not of Butler's making. The symbiont's generating it inside her, and good thing the two punks got to her when they did. She'll have been feeling it for some time, since the incision in her side, and it seems to have sped up after the stitches tore. It's a wonder she managed to drive.

It's a wonder anything about her, really. When he got the text message from the punks and went to retrieve her, he braced himself with a reminder that she has responded differently to the treatment, but it didn't stifle his amazement at her condition.

Butler pulls his hands out from her chest cavity, shakes them off over the plastic. Gloves might be best for this, but he isn't after all a surgeon, and it helps to be able to feel for differences in texture. Katherine's been tested thoroughly. He sent her blood off and got the report and knows he's not in any danger from it. It's not entirely human anymore, but at the blood level at least the symbiont isn't contagious.

Her breath hitches and she sighs but doesn't move. Butler wipes his hands on the plastic. Picks up forceps and a small flashlight. The flesh over Katherine's ribcage lifts easily. The stench confirms what he felt in there. She should be ready.

Butler peels the flesh as far as he dares, shifts his shoes

to avoid the drippings. He's not certain why the subjects' blood always runs thin at this point. Katherine's ribcage is shrunken and yellow and cracking in the sides of her chest cavity, like something shriveled in the sun, replaced by a hard black sac folded to the contours of the displaced bones. Butler nods and traces the forceps over the sac. Frowns.

Thin fibrous membranes stick to the forceps, still running from the sac to the brittle ribs. Butler pushes at them, but they don't detach. He sets the forceps down and takes a step back. He has to think. The membranes should be releasing by now. By all signs Katherine is ready, but the sac is still firmly in place. Something is wrong.

Maybe it was in the blood work, something the Institute missed. But that can't be it. He confirmed the tests himself, to the best of his ability, and if his lab is a bit ad-hoc it's certainly a step up from the motel. The motel, which has housekeeping staff and maintenance, neighbors who might see something.

No cameras at least.

But, no, it can't be her blood. Butler picks up the forceps and peels back the skin for another look and a booming knock at the door sends a jolt through his hands and down the forceps and into Katherine's body.

He stands there for an endless second, shaking with the effort of staying still. Katherine doesn't move, but the sac does. It writhes, and Butler thinks of the ocean again, but the ocean as it will be left one day if the symbiont finds its way into the world before he finds a cure, reflecting no light and clutching oily to the surface of the planet.

Not if he can help it.

He pulls the forceps out, slowly. Holding his breath. The sac roils some more and slows. Nothing leaks out. Good. He doesn't know what would happen if its develop-

ment were interrupted, and this room isn't the place to
find out.

The next knock is longer, deliberate. Whoever it is isn't
going away. Butler looks over the room, how not ready for
guests it is. But the knocking will eventually draw attention,
if it hasn't already.

Butler curses, folds the forceps back against the inside
of his forearm like a fighting knife. Takes long steps to the
door as quietly as he can. Pulls the door until the chain
clinks taught.

As soon as it's open the door slams wider. The base of
the chain tears out of the wall easy, like maybe it's not the
first time. The door catches the corner of Butler's face and
he reels. Footsteps come through the door. Butler raises
his hands to his face, presses them over the contusion
already growing, realizing too late he's showing the
forceps now.

Confident fingers pluck them from his grip. The door
closes and the bolt turns.

Butler removes his hands to see the punk chick with the
Russian name and the lout who follows her around. Cortland. He's the one who would have done the kicking. He's
clutching at his leg, now, new blood seeping through a
bandage.

They waited after their drop-off, followed him here.
Took the time to patch up Cortland and then got impatient.

Butler gathers himself, steps between the intruders and
Katherine. "Do you have any idea what you—what could
have—"

"Can it." Anja lifts a revolver in her hand and lets it
settle back to her side, doesn't need to be aiming it to make a
point. "We came to get paid."

"We discussed this. You're to be paid tomorrow."

"After you've skipped town, yeah, I'm sure. Let me rephrase that."

"You misunderstand."

"We're here to *actually* get paid."

"I took a fucking bullet, man," Cortland whines from next to the door.

Butler nods, holds up his hands. "Yes, okay, so you're agitated."

"I'm fucking *shot*."

"You're shot. Okay. Fine. You're going to get paid, and obviously you don't have any trouble finding me. So, if you don't mind..."

The gun comes up now, Anja's face bored behind it. "Yeah, we mind. This point, I'd feel just about as good plugging you as walking out with the money." She looks to the body on the bed for the first time, doesn't react.

Butler's impressed.

"But, whatever it is you're doing here—and I'm not asking—you need to think whether you want people to come running right now. If there was some sort of disturbance."

Butler nods, frowning, trying to look like he's thinking. He's not. He made up his mind when he saw who it was. The time frame is delicate, and they've likely nudged him closer to the edge of catastrophe. And there's no telling how closed they can really keep their mouths. Sight unseen, sure, but they've come to the motel room, have seen his work.

"I'll get it, then. And you'll be on your way."

He walks to the closet and gets his hands in his suitcase before Cortland thinks better of it and pushes off the wall, shouting and hobbling toward him. Butler holds the envelope of cash out behind him until Cortland slows to take it, then whirls around with the knife, still stooped over. Cortland's stomach swallows the blade, gives it back with a sucking sound.

Anja's gun shouts all the sound from the room. Cortland twitches, slumps onto Butler. Butler heaves him backward into Anja. The gun thuds on the carpet. Anja glances off the bed and onto the floor, envelope in one hand, the other clutching the plastic bedsheet, dragging it down with her.

Butler tries to lunge in a couple directions at once. Winds up standing still. Katherine tumbles down on top of Anja.

Burst of black fluid and Anja's composure finally breaks. She screams and pulls herself out from under and scrambles toward the door, but it's closed and bolted. The black fluid's smeared in a trail from her to Katherine and she slips in it trying to get to her feet and then Butler's on her with the knife.

The knife finds her shoulder and she punches Butler in the neck. He chokes and spits. She swings again and opens the skin above his eye.

Katherine's flesh tears, wet and loud. Anja gets herself upright. Butler's not watching her anymore, is looking instead at the burst sac twitching its way out of Katherine's body, bony limbs shaped like ribs slicing through the membrane and scraping across the floor and plunging deep into Anja's leg. She draws the air to scream but doesn't get it out. Spends the air instead on hauling herself out of the room, dragging the symbiont with her, clutching the money as a reflex more than anything conscious.

Butler finds his feet. Has to come to grips with what's happened here. Will need a few moments he doesn't have. Katherine lies in a pool of viscera and much worse atop the plastic sheet. Cortland moans from the closet. The night's up in flames, and it's time to cut losses.

He drops the driver's license he used to sign for the room in a trash can on the second floor.

AT A BAR that feels much further north of campus than it is, the sun's been down a couple hours already when a man named Bill steps out to the front porch, but the heat's still shimmering its way up off the asphalt. He cracks the tab the bartender knows not to do for him, slurps the foam off the top of the can. He's well on his way to getting a little shimmer of his own going.

As without, so within, is the idea now. Best to match one's surroundings.

And, that beer tab: it's a little a matter of pride, yes. Day he gets too feeble he needs a pimpled fuck with soft hands and a mechanic's shirt to open a beer for him, just put him out to pasture.

Bill's gone to live on a farm, kids. A farm where all the old drunks go. He's happier now, really.

The bar's a house, or used to be. Purple paint still bright but peeling, guitar shop upstairs, beer and wine downstairs. Anybody's guess how the city council got it in their heads to zone it commercial, but Bill knows the owner, has a hunch on that score.

Bill smiles with his lips, swishes his beer hard through his teeth.

What he's doing, other than digging how the evening air feels when there's no work tomorrow, is giving a fellow inside a few minutes to cool himself off, if the guy wants to take it.

If not, well. Bill does have some idea how to cool a person down.

He quits toying with the beer and lets the last half of it drain straight down his throat. Like scratching an itch.

Bill takes a quick breath to get the blood going and stops himself from pitching the empty can at the shrubbery, balances it on the porch railing instead. Fuck it, kid's had enough time. And anyway, Bill needs another beer.

He pushes through the front door into what used to be a living room. Trails his finger through the frost on the gas-station-style coolers on the wall opposite the bar. The kid at the end of the bar picks up his beer. Doesn't look Bill's way, just sidles out through the back room toward the patio.

Bill smiles and takes the vacated seat. College boys ought to keep themselves out back. Except maybe for the one behind the bar, already sliding a fresh can to Bill. That one's okay.

Bill cracks the can. Everything's where it should be, and he sets to helping the night along. A gaggle comes through the door and lines up for the bartender's attention.

And a scream comes from the patio.

Bill winces, waits for an amateur drunk to come careening through, but no one does. A second scream, louder and shorter. The bartender's trying to hear three orders simultaneously. He looks out back, but the other bartender went on her break, or is sneaking one.

Bill tips his beer back, doesn't put it down until it's empty. "Hey, son. Want I should go see what's what?"

"Yeah, thanks."

He slides another can across to Bill and pointedly forgets to ask for money.

Bill strolls through the back room, where no one's moved. The patio's a cluster of people, though, around a chair in the corner by the fence. Tension vibrating magnetic and Bill wades into the pool of bodies. Elbows his way to the chair.

It's the kid from inside, the one who'd stomped in like he owned the place. Bill can't hold it against the bar if they're welcoming a younger sort of drinker, gotta pay the bills, but now the punk's standing over this gory puddle of a woman, one hand behind her head like he's shocked at what he's done. Like he wants the last minute or two back. Yeah, and he's gonna want that more. One day people will realize that Bill's usually right when he feels trouble coming.

He takes a last pull on his beer, hard enough it foams up, trickles out from the corners of his mouth. He grabs the kid's shoulder and yanks him upright. Slams the bottom of the can into the kid's forehead. Crumpling aluminum, crescent of blood blooming into a stream. The kid reels into the fence. Raises his hands. Bill takes a fast step forward.

"Whoa whoa whoa," the kid, trying to talk faster than his tongue will quite manage, "what the fuck, I got out of your way, man, there's a *situation* here—"

"Oh, yeah, I see the situation."

Bill slips his fist in under the kid's hands. The kid folds. Everyone on the patio standing paralyzed, a wall of rubber necks.

Bill licks his lips, feeling this. He gets to be the hero for once, set things right the way he's been wanting to. It's a long time coming.

The kid fights his way to his feet. When his eyes go wide, it's not at how Bill's coming in for another round, but behind him, over Bill's shoulder. Bill smiles wider, refuses to fall for it. Winds his hand back, turns his front foot to follow through the punch.

He's aiming for the kid's face, now.

But the swing doesn't come. His arm catches on something, his foot twists with nothing behind it, and Bill drops with a sharp pop in his knee.

His arm doesn't come down with him, though. Hard white tension in his shoulder. Bill looks up, at the dripping hands wrapped around his elbow, stretching that shoulder in a bad-news angle. The hands are all he can see at first, like they've materialized out of air to clamp down and fuck up his moment.

Then the face comes in. Blond hair stringing through the dirt dusted over blood, head cocked at a curious angle. She's looking at his hand. Sniffing. Her tongue darts out, sandpaper-rough over Bill's palm.

Bill's stomach leaps into his throat. The woman's eyes flick straight into his face. The features twist into something like a sneer, but too much, like the muscles are imprecise and unused to the work of facial expressions. The shadows thrown by the porch light sink crevasses into her cheeks.

She licks at his hand again and he rips it away, falls the rest of the way down. The kid behind her shuffles to his feet. Her head whips that way.

She's standing hunched over from above the waist, and when she takes a step toward the kid her torso sways a little, not held in place right, having to catch up to her legs as she moves. Not looking as much like she needs saving.

"Hey, can you hear me?" the kid says. "We should get you to a hospital."

She dives for him. White teeth find flannel and the kid just stares down at her, clamped onto his shirt, until she jerks her head like stop-motion video and those teeth go red.

The kid shouts and scrambles back, but she's locked on tight. She chomps down again, again, and she's impossibly worked a hole through the shirt. Fresh blood running down her chin.

Bill uses a nearby table to crutch himself to his feet and reaches out to grab her shoulder but she falls off on her own. She runs shocked hands over her lips, turns and spits until there's nothing left in her mouth. She turns and looks Bill in the face, and she doesn't come up past his gut, the way she's standing.

She sprays vomit, flesh and bile and a smell like the swamp in July, warm and heavy on Bill's pants. Cocks her head to the sky, sniffing.

"Hey, now, what in the hell—"

The woman surges past him, hands clawing for his face, feet stuttering. Bill takes a good rake to the cheek and stumbles over a chair, crashes to the concrete. The woman bursts through the wall of onlookers and scrambles over the fence, into the night. Leaves the wood stained where she's climbed.

Bill curses and lifts himself up. The kid's propped up on a table, looking at his wounds. They're not so deep as they'd looked, but the bite marks are welling heavy where his shirt used to cover.

"Hey," Bill said. "Might wanna get to a hospital. That shit, people's mouths? It'll infect sure as you're born."

"Uh huh. You're very helpful."

"Hey, I misread the situation. You do come off like a bit of a shit."

The kid makes wide eyes at him. Forehead dripping, shirt sticking to his skin with the evening's injuries.

"Anyway, at least you were further from her when she

took her chompers to you than you might have been. I got that right, didn't I?"

The kid smiles, and Bill thinks maybe he's okay, after all, and then the kid whips his arm around, catches a half-full beer bottle on the way. The glass breaks over Bill's head and he goes down again in a rain of foam and glass.

THE COUNTY CLERK gets up the same time she always does, sun only just starting to redden the sky, and remembers with a quick internal curse that she hasn't taken the trash out. There's a half-full bag in the can, another full to bursting but tied off sitting next to it.

She looks out the window. The neighbor's trash doesn't look to be empty. Maybe this rare lapse will pass without consequence.

The county clerk loops one hand through the bag on the floor and grabs both of plastic loops of the bag in the can in the other, tugs it up. It doesn't really tighten the way she wants but soon it won't be her problem.

She hauls it up and shifts it to her left hand, uses the right to open the latch on the side door. Sees her trash can tipped over on its side before she gets down the three steps and takes a deep breath.

The neighborhood is an improvement over her last place, enough to keep her here the last three years, but racoons have been a problem.

She takes the lighter of the bags in her right hand and slings it over her shoulder, noting that it finally cinches closed the way she wanted, and whips it at her toppled trash can. It hangs in the air and spins a couple times and lands on something.

Not ground. Not trash can.

A snarl and a shuffling of plastic and something rears up behind her trash can, trailing plastic wrappers and vegetable cuttings.

No, some*one*. Onion peels and banana peels in her hair.

The county clerk draws breath to shout but the person only watches her. Maintains eyes contact and reaches down to her bloodstained shirt, scoops up a handful of carrot shavings and tests them with her teeth tentatively. Just to see.

Spits them out viciously.

There's something wrong with her chest. The county clerk wants to help, but it's too early in the morning and she didn't sign up for this, not at her front door, but before she can even remember where her cell phone is the bloodied trash-eater hooks her nose up to the sky, and then east, like she's located what she's looking for by smell alone, and lopes off.

ANJA DRIVES. The thing clamped to her left foot hurts terribly, blurs her vision and floods her head with the smell of lightning, until it doesn't anymore. A warm numbness spreads from her calf to her toes, her waist, and the leg is so much dead weight. At least it's her left leg, and she can still work the pedals.

But she remembers where the thing came from, bursting from the body of the woman she and Cortland delivered.

She remembers the way the woman smelled with this thing growing inside her.

She passed out in the car a couple blocks from the motel, woke up far too long later. No telling what could have happened while she was out, but she's got a full tank of gas and can get just about anywhere she needs to go. Has no idea where that could be, though. Hospitals are probably not going to be the most helpful, not until she gets the thing off of her. Somewhere private, then, with some pliers and ideally some painkillers. But the last was more Cortland's department.

And the leg's numbness is threatening to spread, warm streaks running up through her body. It'll have to be whiskey, then. The sun's high up already, putting its sharp edge on things, which means there ought to be a liquor store open.

With Cortland's share of the pay, she's got plenty to get out of town on. Can't wait to do it.

Five minutes later she wheels across the oncoming lane into a liquor store parking lot. The place is teeming. A couple college kids out front smoking, looking around in a way that's trying real hard to be natural. Their buddy surely inside, fake ID or the only one of age. A car pulls up next to her and a couple gets out, carrying an empty case of wine to fill up.

Anja looks at the bony thing clutching her leg, so hardened it looks damp, digging deeper into her and absorbing all the light. Her pants won't quite cover it, no matter how she shifts around, and no way is she going to reach down and pull it over, risk touching the thing.

She tries not to think about what it might be doing to her body, about the way the woman felt. The tacky flesh, the smell of rot. The blazing-hot skin squirming, the icy breath.

Whatever that Butler's gotten her into, it's keeping her out of sight for the foreseeable future.

The liquor store, though, has a drive-through window. Anja thinks about Florida again, wonders if it has a sense of humor about itself after all.

She puts the car in park at the window, crosses her good leg over the other one, asks for a fifth of something fucking cheap. The clerk raises his eyebrow, doesn't have the time or inclination to try to read her mind.

Anja grinds her teeth and asks for the first thing she can see on the shelf inside. The clerk hands it over and she shoves some money at him, waits for him to fumble with the register.

She's about to pull away when a quick flash of motion from the bushes draws her eye. Bloodied and stooped, and she can't be seeing what she's seeing. The clerk clears his throat, holds out the money to her. She nods and mumbles, and when she turns her head again there's nothing there. She rubs her palms against her eyes and pulls away.

The roads blink past, and there's only one place for her to go. When Butler hired them, he gave her the key to a storage unit out past the edge of town, one unit in a largely unmonitored facility. No doubt he'll be checking it out, changing the locks before long, but it's the only place she can think of. And she can feel herself fading, getting weaker. She needs to go to ground and soon.

The traffic's murder near the college so she breaks off from it, wanders some little surface roads until there's some breathing room. The road narrows and winds through brush and widens into a highway. She's missed the storage unit. She curses and stomps on the brake, pulls a very illegal u-turn. Flurry of horns but no sirens. She retraces her path and sure enough the facility comes up on the right.

She breathes, breathes. Eases past the empty security booth and pulls up in front of the unit. She parks but thinks better of it, finally stops a half-row down and on the other side. Sunlight glints off the blue steel doors and she gets a little faint, steps into the glare and shades her eyes and hunches over walking to the door like that'll help. The key won't go into the lock. Fingers like rubber. Sweat jumping out to the surface of her skin. She sets the whiskey on the concrete and two-hands the key home. Fades almost to black heaving the door up. Turns around for the bottle and something blocks a long shadow over her.

She looks up in time to register a dirty face with hair matted to it rushing toward her, a contorted body behind, leaning too low to the ground. The woman from the field, the drop-off, the motel room, somehow not dead despite looking the part. Pressing her hands to her chest, *into* her chest, and rushing into the storage unit.

Anja steps back, not even thinking about it, and the door ratchets all the way down with both of them inside. The woman hisses and Anja raises her hands to protect her face, but the woman's not aiming there. She drops down and seizes Anja's bad leg, yanks. The force upsets the delicate balance of her body and her torso folds to the side with Anja's leg. Anja slips back and falls through clouds to the concrete floor. Doesn't even feel the impact. The storage unit swims.

The woman clutches Anja's leg. Her lower body is sitting, legs under her like the primmest debutante, her upper torso nearly horizontal. Something gossamer and slick and foul connecting the two.

Anja can't move. Numb body and warm, a feeling like falling.

The woman runs her teeth over the skin of Anja's leg, failing to get purchase. She finally pauses to take aim and bites. Anja distantly feels the puncture. The woman slurps hard but stops fast, spitting Anja's flesh back onto her leg. Doesn't like how Anja tastes, apparently.

Some maniac part of Anja's brain, way back, cackles.

The creature on Anja's leg thrusts its legs in sequence, like running. The pain breaks through again and, on its heels, a gaping nothing of the senses.

The woman looks at the creature. Intently. Crookedly. She leans forward waiting for more movement. Sniffs. Some unholy cousin of a smile rends cracks in the dried blood around her mouth.

TWO

THERE'S TWO PEOPLE WAITING IN THE PLASMA CENTER
office already, eyeing each other cagily, trying to look like
they're not looking. Janet reads the paper at the front desk.
She's already told them she can't do anything until the tech
gets here. She's just a clerk. It's true. They don't let first-year
nursing *students* do anything with needles, even in a shit-
hole like this.

Just a couple years and it'll be a different job, this whole
scene a bad dream.

For now, though, it's the daily grind of poverty,
harvesting people's blood for a pittance, business heavier at
the end of the month when the EBT's run out.

She grinds her teeth. The front page of the paper is a
body count above the fold, the jobless rate below. She
supposes she should feel lucky.

Yeah, lucky. She's on the giving end of the desperation
needle. A banner year.

"When's he get here?" one of the men asks for the fifth
time.

23

"Fifteen minutes ago." Janet shrugs. "How do I know? Maybe he's caught in traffic."

The man opens his mouth and Janet braces for a scene, but the door swings open and the phlebotomist comes in, worse for wear. The right side of his face is a concussion sunset, purple and yellow under sunglasses.

"Jesus, Butler, where've you been? What happened?"

He shrugs it off. "Took a tumble last night. Guess I'm a little slow." He motions to the first man in the waiting room. "Let's go."

And naturally the man following Butler to the chair shoots daggers at *her*, not him, probably regretting the missed chance to lay into her.

She brings Butler a needle from the back, the first one she lays hands on.

He takes it, frowns. "No, the first one. It's marked in orange."

She sighs. "Good god, what does it matter?"

"They're *ordered*, Janet. So we can track them? Inventory, blood type. For the screening. We've covered this."

She goes to get him the one he wants, hears him singsong over his shoulder that they have important work to do.

DANI CAN TYPE PRETTY FAST, but not as fast as the financial planner piping in her headphones likes to talk. She's gotten jobs from him before, and every time she has to lift her foot off the pedal to stop the recording, with each little dent into the productivity score that'll be taped to the back wall of the office tomorrow, she dreams of driving to his Illinois suburb, torching some strip-mall office. Instead of dreaming of burning the one she's sitting in.

It doesn't help her type faster, just harder.

The bastard buzzes his car window down, letting traffic noise wash over the recording. Dani pictures him at a stoplight, talking into an earpiece like the forceful and busy Type-A conqueror he's trying to be, and relishes the key sequence for *garbled*. Sends the job and logs off.

Maybe some of it was intelligible after that. If quality control catches it, she'll find out.

Dani clunks her headphone on the desk and stands up. The cheap-keyboard hornet buzz of the office comes in, carries her down the aisle between two office-length desks of computer workstations and out the front door.

It's making her shift longer. The clock stops when you take a break, but at least the door swinging shut takes the clacking with it, and the smell of old carpet and instant coffee.

She drums her fingers on her jeans, bums a smoke off the guy whose name she can't remember who's staring off across the parking lot. He hands her his lighter and she blows smoke. A truck pulls up, no one she recognizes, and drops someone off at the plasma center next door.

It's a long beige shopping center with an extremely optimistic parking lot. SpeakScript doesn't have a sign except on the front door's tinted window. The company website has almost no information on it, but it does mention how that tinted glass protects the customers' privacy, like someone might be peeking through to try and steal details of a whole-life insurance sales meeting.

To one side of SpeakScript, a dead slot. Logos from a few failed businesses all peeking through each other where they've been incompletely torn off. Then an art-supplies place, the largest spot and on the corner. Dani's never seen anyone in there but it's been there forever, must catch the discount business from the university.

Past that, on the corner, the folding table the old church lady uses. She'll give you lunch for free every other weekday, but you'll have to endure a sermon about keeping yourself out of jail before anything gets scooped onto the paper plates. Dani's availed herself once or twice, but it just made her feel sad, not full.

To the other side, the plasma center. That one doesn't have a sign beyond the door logo, either.

Dani wonders how much of the rest of her day's pay she could make up if she blew off those hours and stopped by there, sold a different part of herself instead. The second drag starts to scratch the itch in her blood. She breathes out through her nose, reaches the lighter back to its owner. Finally turns to where Cora's glaring holes in her back.

"You looking for a job?" Dani says.

"No. I need to talk to you."

Cora wrinkles her nose at Dani's smoke. Dani puffs a blithe lungful, watches it hang between them in the humidity.

"I don't suppose," stepping out of the cloud, "that you've seen Katherine lately."

"Don't remember offhand, Cora. I'd have to check my appointment book."

"Do I look like I'm fucking around?"

"You never do." Dani takes a long enough drag that it's not quite even enjoyable and grinds her smoke out on the sole of her shoe, stashes it in her watch pocket for later. "Not for a couple days. Didn't come in yesterday."

"She didn't come home last night."

Dani stops, one hand already on the door. "Sorry for your troubles." It even comes out halfway friendly.

It doesn't take. "The fuck do you know about our troubles? Who said we had troubles?"

"Okay." Dani turns, sharp. Catches herself. "What is it, then?"

Cora's eyes flare, shift their focus. Dani hears the guy who bummed her a smoke pass behind them and go inside. Cora's eyes settle back on her.

Dani just holds steady. "All clear, now?"

Her voice creeps high enough that the kids smoking and sitting on the curb look over. They try not to, which just makes it more obvious.

"I just want to know," Cora stage-whispers, "what y'all got up to last night."

"'Y'all.' Well, *I* went to Nelly's, started tying one on. Then I left the bar and walked home and finished tying it."

"'Tying one on.'"

"Yep." Dani looks back at the SpeakScript door, at the explanation that ought to be.

"Think your boyfriend..."

Dani laughs. "Cry on Kyle's shoulder if you want, but we haven't been together in a while."

Cora flushes.

"Look," Dani says. "You asked, I told you. I think I get how things look to you, sometimes. Maybe. But I really haven't seen her."

A girl Dani knows to say hi to wanders out of the plasma center, orange bandage around her elbow. She nods to Dani and walks on through this little moment, a little unsteady. In ten minutes, Dani will see the ambulance pull up for her, to carry her out on a stretcher from where she's fainted outside the SpeakScript bathroom.

Now, the girl lights the smoke that, with her thinned blood, will help put her there, and walks a polite distance from the faces Dani and Cora are making at each other.

"Hey," Cora says. She puts a little confessional quaver in her voice, the kind that must work so well with Katherine, to keep her from making an honest break of it. "You hear from her, you gimme a call, okay?"

Dani can't quite keep from it, call it old friends, but she lets her voice get reassuring. "Yeah, I'll do that."

Cora walks backward a few steps and nods and turns away quick.

Dani fishes the bummed butt up from her pocket, has to borrow a lighter from the girl, already heading in and looking pale. Dani tries to ignore the weird barbecue smell of a stubbed-out smoke and lights it. She mutters *back to the word mines*, but there's nobody listening, and it's an old joke, and she's not ready to get back to work yet anyway.

Dani winds up spending the night at Kyle's apartment, the way it happens sometimes, and Cora actually does call him in the morning. Kyle takes it better than Dani would have thought. He's grown more of a sense of humor since they broke up. He tells her to ignore her, not to get involved. That Cora is just doing what Cora does, and if Katherine never comes to her senses, Dani can't put it on herself.

It's good advice and she takes it in. Thinks it over, nods seriously. Kisses him and gets dressed and walks calmly down the stairs and drives to Cora and Katherine's house.

Cora's car is in the driveway, so Dani parks down the

street. Cora works afternoons usually, and she doesn't disappoint now. Comes out in her barista apron, hurried and focused. She pulls out and drives away. Dani pulls across the street from the house and gets out.

She doesn't have a key, but she does know about the little door on the side of the house, opening from the laundry room, that Katherine never locks. And Cora wouldn't touch laundry to save her mother. Dani lets herself in and rummages around the bedroom until she finds the laptop in the desk drawer.

The normal thing to do would be to ask Cora to track Katherine's phone. There's no particular reason she couldn't just tell Cora, but she didn't really think the computer would be here, either. It makes her stomach sink, means that Katherine hasn't just cut all ties and relocated.

But Katherine wouldn't have told Cora her password, probably. Not after the email incident. Dani knows it, though. *Sheryl Crow* with some numbers for letters, same as all of Katherine's new passwords, the kind of music she'd never admit to liking sober. Dani logs in and finds the find-my-phone program, hopes that Katherine's set it up. The computer wheezes and putters. Dani thinks it's a lost cause and puts her hand on the monitor to close the laptop, but then there's a faint mechanical ding. Red dot on a map, no place Dani recognizes.

She squints. It's way out on the edge of town, by where University Ave bends off into a highway north. It doesn't make any sense. There's no place Katherine could be living out there, nothing but the industrial farming remnants clinging to edge of this college town. She gets a pen from the desk and writes the address on her wrist.

It's a long drive, for Palm Gulf, clear on the opposite end of the city. Dani takes the long way around, past the townie bars and the carefully cute little neighborhood with benches along its retention ponds. The buildings get smaller and the grass more aggressive, and a little storage facility peeks up through the encroaching wilderness.

Dani pulls in. Yellow concrete walls and blue metal doors. There's no sign of life in the first two rows. She circles around to the last one, hope fading. One car at the end of the row, a brown and white station wagon. Dani parks next to it and takes a deep breath. Gets out of the car, pounds on the nearest locker door. It rattles against its track. Silence. Dani looks side to side, pounds again, harder. Nothing.

She gives up and gets her car door open, but something glints in the sun. Dani shields her eyes and squints and can just make out a plastic fifth of alleged whiskey, set on the ground next to a unit several doors down. She looks around again. Nobody in sight.

A shuffling sound from the unit grows as she gets closer. She puts her ear to the door but can't make sense of it. She raises her fist, considers. The padlock's open on the ground. She decides to knock. The motion inside quickens in response, settles back down.

"Katherine?"

Mumbling. Dani's chest thumps.

"*Kath*erine. It's me, yeah? Dani. Cora's not with me, okay? Just let me in."

Something slides and falls over inside. Dani has had enough, grabs the bottom of the door and opens it on an abattoir.

The smell inside pushes her physically away. Her first thought is of some animals locked inside, finally getting hungry enough to tear each other apart, leave that rotting smell in the unit, but she makes out a figure in the shadows.

Hunched over another one. She shakes her head, telling herself not to, and takes a step inside.

There's a woman sprawled on the floor, calf pincushioned by the legs of something like a giant spider and oozing where some of the limbs have been yanked out. The woman shakes against the concrete, then lies still. Shakes again every couple seconds, like her body's trying to get booted up and not having an easy time of it.

Two hands press down on the spider-thing. Katherine's face hovering just above.

Dani gasps and lets the door ratchet down and clang shut behind her. She rushes to Katherine, but she's surely too late; as she gets close, she how Katherine's folded over from somewhere near her sternum, more like the posture of a body after a long fall than sitting. Blood pooling in the crater of her shirt, drying out along the edges.

"God, what happened?"

She puts her hand on Katherine's face, jerks back at the warmth still there. Katherine looks over to her and leans down again to the spider thing.

Dani sees the parts of it missing, the sickly green dripping there. The same color as the area around Katherine's lips. She shakes her head, no, no, but it's happening.

Katherine works her teeth in under the thing's carapace, worries out a chunk of flesh. Swallows. Breathes hard, like the stuff is giving her life, but Dani can smell it.

"I," Katherine's voice, all wrong, "I need." Long pause, meat half-chewed and dripping. "Dani."

Dani's mouth opens, but she has nothing for this.

"I...I need..."

Katherine leans down to the creature again, grips it in her teeth, and Dani reaches for her before she knows what she's doing. Grabs her hair. Has to stop this.

Katherine moans, shouts. The thing, one leg still in her mouth, flails its other legs around angrily. One leg jabs into Dani's wrist and presses her arm to the wall. Katherine takes another bite and the thing lies quiet.

Through mounting shock Dani thinks it looks like a contented dog, lying in its owner's lap.

THE LIGHTS in the plasma center have been off for hours. The front room is dark, late afternoon sunlight seeping only dimly through the frosted glass. No reason to attract attention from the typing hipsters next door. Butler hunches over his workstation in the back room. It's not exactly standard for a plasma center to have this much equipment on-site, or this type. Strictly speaking, they shouldn't be dealing with actual blood, with whole blood. That's done off-site, where the company that owns the center does the screening for diseases and abnormalities.

This is an unofficial operation, though, kept in an unmarked drawer in a filing cabinet next to his desk, in a padlocked but worn-looking metal box that, from the outside, might well store hand tools for the odd repair around the office. On the inside, though, it's tight and clean, rows of black ampules along the top tier, syringes and swabs and rubbing alcohol in the middle, various measuring instruments on the bottom.

Butler takes an ampule and a syringe from the box. He loads a few drops of the black liquid from the ampule, careful to keep it settled at the very tip of the needle.

He reaches into the plastic drawer where they keep the

32

needles for drawing plasma and finds one wrapped in orange. They're kept carefully marked and ordered, he makes certain of that. The black fluid takes a minute to start to trickle out of the first needle. It always takes just a touch more pressure than it seems like it should, as though up to a certain point the liquid grows more viscous and then gives. Once the trickle starts, it patters and then spurts into the new vessel, which he holds horizontally.

As soon as the load is deposited, he quickly moves it under the desk, out of the light. It dries so surprisingly quickly. Butler rolls the syringe around in his fingers, following a series of patterns designed to make an even coat. He pulls it out and checks that the whole of the glass has turned the right slight shade of gray. Twists the overhead light to shine directly down and holds the syringe close to the blazing bulb, turning it some more.

In a matter of seconds, the liquid on the marked syringe has dried to a transparent sheen that's only visible at certain angles, if it catches the light just right.

Butler inspects it and returns it to its place in the ordered sequence in the plastic drawer. It will do for the next patient on his list, but he remembers how many treatments he's administered, how often it doesn't take. Sometimes they don't react to it much at all, their bodies fighting off the influence before anything can grow, and sometimes it grows all wrong. Too fast or to slow, or along corridors of the body not conducive to such invasion.

This most recent one was a breakthrough. The most promising he's seen since he was recruited into the project. The lack of containment and her escape have set him back, taken his best chance.

He switches off his desk lamp and leaves through the back door.

THE DOOR to the storage unit shakes slowly. Rocks up against the limits of its track, then clatters back down. The empty parking lot doesn't notice. Inside the storage unit is a skittering, a too-fast drawing of breath. The door creaks up an inch and falls back down. Up again, a little farther, then jolts upward all at once. What might well be a woman tumbles through, all wrong angles and dripping.

She rights herself and reaches back into the unit. Mouth forming silent vowels. Pulls a foot in each hand and drags her friend, whose name she can't remember, whose taste she can, out into the late afternoon.

Her friend's breathing gets faster, shallower, until her head knocks against the concrete outside and she's for a moment terrifyingly still.

The dripping woman drops the feet, raises her hands in cartoon alarm. Remembers finally the feeling of a motion more than its purpose and folds over at the waist to hook her hands under her friend's arms.

To anyone passing on the road long minutes later, they'll look like after-work drinks gone too long, one friend easing the other home.

IT'S BEEN seven days since Cora replaced the laundry-room doorknob. She came home from work and found it open, thought that maybe Katherine had gotten over her tantrum and come home. She hadn't even known they'd been fighting, had thought things were getting better, so maybe Katherine just needed a few days. But there was no one in the little house, and it was only after she'd gone through all the rooms that the fear of an intruder hit her and, having already checked everywhere, she had no outlet for the twitching adrenaline, the invasive feeling of a shadow in her home.

So she got back in her car and went to the hardware store.

It was the kind of job that Katherine would usually have insisted on doing. She'd say it was because she liked to do things with her hands besides type sometimes, but Cora has long suspected that it was more she didn't trust Cora to do it. Cora left the screwdriver and doorknob bubble-pack on top of the washing machine after she'd installed it.

Katherine hadn't been sleeping at home for a few days, most of a week, but she'd still found ways to make her presence known. She'd show up in the evening to pick up something she needed, something she forgot. They wouldn't talk really, but Cora appreciated the appearance for the gesture it was. Katherine was making it clear she wasn't gone for good, at least not yet. Needed some time and some space but was still in orbit, still breathing some of the same air as Cora. Probably was just holed up with friends and would come back when she'd cooled off.

That stopped a couple days ago.

Now she sits in her car in the SpeakScript parking lot, watching the people on breaks outside. They huddle in circles laughing off the monotony or sit against the wall with a cigarette. She wasn't expecting this many of the faces to be unfamiliar, but the SpeakScript turnover is famous. For every twenty people they hire, maybe two will still be working there after a couple weeks.

Cora had once made it most of a week before the coffee shop called, had someone quit and needed a replacement, and she never came back. Couldn't really understand why anyone would suffer here when there are places that have tip jars.

There were some old timers, though, people who'd worked there for years, getting into some kind of groove Cora couldn't understand with the voices droning through the headphones, some sort of minor magic protecting their wrists from carpal tunnel.

One of these comes out, tall and with stringy hair, and Cora's sure she's met him before but can't come up with his name. He's holding a check out in front of him, flicking its edge with his finger and sauntering off to the bank, and Cora can't think of a single reason he would talk to her.

Really, no one here will. Short of spotting Katherine herself, there's nothing to be done here except sit and stare. Better to think of another spot of Katherine's and try there, maybe run into her.

The list of places Katherine might go to lie low might be sizeable, but most of it would be obscure to Cora. She's never quite gotten along with most of Katherine's friends, the art-school kids who never quite made it to art school, and has spent the couple years since they moved in together begging off from concerts and parties.

She hopes Katherine's just lying a little lower than usual. That would be one thing. Probably after a certain amount of trying to raise her, she would give up, respect if grudgingly the desire for distance.

But now Katherine hasn't been to work in at least two

days, and if she'd found something new, there would have been celebrating, bordering on gloating.

No, something more than a spat is up. The police don't seem overly worried. If *roommate* didn't exactly bring them around to Cora's concern, *girlfriend* just put the phone-duty cop in mind of some kind of phase, some youthful rebellion Katherine had grown out of and left behind, Cora's concern with it. He told her to call back when her real family could confirm that she was missing.

Cora began to say that she'd been missing to them for nearly a decade, now, gone to hell and the university, but the operator caught something in her tone he didn't like and hung up. She hadn't expected much, but she expected a little more than that.

Jim Jerry's, though, is something of an institution with the worn-denim and cut-off-shirts crowd. It's the only place she can think to go.

The old purple house looks like she remembers it but more ragged. The paint's peeling and the porch has some more broken planks, but she hasn't been here in years, and then only at night. Lovestruck and a little drunk, the place kind of sparkled.

Now she steps over two traveling kids and their sweaty-looking guitar, ignoring whatever burnout greeting they offer when they notice her, into an interior not much cooler than outside. Condensation blurs the labels of all the bottles in the fridges along one wall. A couple daytimers are busy holding down the bar. Cora scans them, finds one bruised but familiar. He hunkers over his beer in the corner, face in darkness but recently battered.

Cora takes the seat next to him and he flinches away, startled from a reverie that was itself interrupting his waiting for someone. The bartender looks at her, at him, at her looking at him. Slouches back to ignore them both.

"Didn't make a friend, there," the guy says.

"Well, I wasn't here to talk to him."

The bartender pushes off his leaning spot by the register, barely pretending to have not been listening. "Get you something, miss?"

"Bud. And one for my friend."

The bartender drifts around the bar to the fridges on the other wall. It would have been faster, probably, for Cora to grab the drinks herself and pay at the register, but the protocol she remembers is you do that if you're sitting in the back room or outside. Sit at the bar, you get your bar tended.

"Gotta say, I remember you from around, but I don't know—"

"Cora. Can't think of yours, either."

"Mitch."

Two beers arrive. Cora pays the man, who drifts back to the register, a little less hostile.

"Thanks," Mitch says.

"No problem. You looked like you could use it." She slides the second bottle out to the edge of her personal space, as far over as possible for it to still look like it's hers. "They're both for you, actually."

"Grazie."

He takes a pull on his bottle, longer now that he knows there's another waiting behind it. The bartender just stares now, eyebrows raised, until Cora nudges Mitch's arm and leads him out to the back porch and into the backyard. Wide slats on a wood fence strung with Christmas lights that snake their way up into the lower fronds of a palm tree, a few iron picnic tables around, all empty. They take the one furthest from the porch.

"There was a thing here, the other night. Last night." He waves to his face. "Thing with a regular."

"But I should see the other guy, right?"

"Believe it or not. It was a weird night. I just fucking hate regulars, man."

"Then why don't you go drink somewhere else?"

He stares at her, then smiles. Good. She's kinda proud of that.

"It was a weird scene, man. I'm surprised you didn't hear about it."

"I'm not the most social creature, Mitch."

"Creature. Yeah," he says and starts to bullshit.

It's a story full of beer and slighted male pride and a couple of sucker punches, something about how people always think Mitch is younger than he is that she doesn't know what she's supposed to do with. She gets why the bartender's frosty, if Mitch really broke a bottle on some good old boy.

Cora's eyes glaze over until he mentions the bloodied woman at the center of it. He starts to describe the other guy getting up, and spitting blood and getting woozy, but Cora holds up her hand.

"Was the girl okay, though?"

"Dunno. She just left."

"What, no one said anything to her inside?"

"No, she never *went* inside."

What she did was clamber over the fence. She was hurt but managed that. Not exactly the Olympics, but a solid six feet while wounded isn't nothing.

"But she was all torn up, you know. Blood every-fuck-ing-where. Like she got cut in the gut, like—" He looks around the empty patio. It's still empty. "Like somebody opened her *up* or something. I don't know."

39

They sit in silence. Mitch even forgets about his beer.

"There's something else," he finally says, picking the label free of the bottle. "I don't know. It was dark, and she was all bloody. Kept her head down, you know, so there was some serious shadow."

"Who?" Stomach tightening, hearing his answer before it comes out.

"It looked a lot like Katherine, man. It looked like her exactly, except I don't think she recognized me."

Cora swallows, wishes she hadn't given him the second beer.

"And the bite...I don't know. It didn't hurt at first, then it did for like half of today. Then it starting healing up real quick. I mean, I thought it was getting infected, but it wasn't. Just felt really wrong."

Cora doesn't have anything to say to that.

BUTLER FOLLOWS the protocol almost giddily. Drives past the university hotel, past the downtown bars, out into unincorporated county land to the falling-down fishing dock. Circles the used-to-be bait store lot once with his headlights on, to draw attention, then again with them off for the second half of the signal.

It felt like spy-movie schtick the first time he did it. It still does, but now it's because of the meeting's content more than its form.

He smiles remembering that first meeting. How he was pretty sure it was university nonsense, somebody looking to get something done for cheap, without the grad students and their noisy union, the headlight routine as much to impart a sense of importance as keep anything secret.

Butler carries no such illusions to this meeting. It's essential that it never gets out what goes on. The supplier he's meeting would probably be protected, or at least have some deniability plan, but Butler's pretty sure that would involve withdrawing their support and that their cover wouldn't extend to him. All the evidence is in the toolbox in the plasma center, simple enough to dispose of, but the project is too important to consider that. The project has to be protected.

The front door swings in before he's out of the car, so he's visible through the screen door. The floodlights click on; he's spotlit but can't see into the dark shack. He swallows. It's a naked feeling you don't get used to. He holds his hands out to the side, briefcase dangling from one of them. Walks up very slowly, stands in front of the screen.

One set of hands pushes the screen aside. Another presents itself calmly for the briefcase, which Butler hands over.

The hands click the case open and briefly check the nothing inside of it. Perfunctorily pass the fingertips along the lining and then White comes forward to hand it back.

Butler takes it. "No problems?"

"Of course."

Butler follows him inside.

Butler doesn't know the other man there, the screen-holder, but he leaves White and Butler alone. White's got a purple polo shirt tucked into pressed khaki shorts, neon-green Fightin' Turtle on the chest. His tan is impressive for a man who supervises a lab. Butler wonders whether he's replaced some of the fluorescent lights there with tanning bulbs, figures that would muck up drug research. Maybe some supervisors are by proxy, able to spend most of their time outside.

The inside of the bait shop is still ready for business, if decayingly so. Tackle and bait and buckets on the couple shelves, some old poles leaned behind the counter. Empty plastic jugs near the register lined with earthworm-dirt residue. A card table has been set up in the middle of the floor, with two chairs and an electric lantern. White takes one seat, waves Butler into the other.

"What happened last night?"

Butler stammers; White is usually less direct. "It's under control. I hired a—"

"I do not know anything about that." White stares until he gets a nod back, clears his throat. "We received your message. Our retrieval team removed one body but did not recover the subject."

"They...what? Why?"

"It seems the subject was not there to be recovered."

"There's no way that the patient—"

"Subject."

"That the subject left on her own power."

"I was under that impression as well."

Butler twists his pinky between the fingers of his other hand and stops, annoyed at having fidgeted. "Then I don't know. I don't know what happened."

"This was your most promising subject, correct?"

"Yes. I mean, there are others, of course, and progressing, but..."

"But none as far along."

There's no point in soft-selling it. "Not even close."

"Then this is a setback," White says. "But not a complete one, necessarily, if the subject can be recovered. Do we know why this subject has progressed quickly?"

"It may have to do with closer monitoring. She comes to the clinic regularly, at more or less predictable intervals, but more frequently of late. Perhaps by checking more often we've changed the development."

"It could also have to do with some unauthorized modifications you've made to the procedure, in this case. Dosages, for example."

Butler opens his mouth and decides to nod instead.

"And those modifications will have interacted with her biology in ways we will need to study her to understand."

"It's an experimental procedure..."

"And we cannot study her if we cannot find her."

Butler waits for more. It doesn't come. "I'll find her."

"Good. Call the Institute when you have, and we will send a team. In the meantime, do you have the next subject ready?"

"Of course. I have a next candidate lined up. He's made repeat contact and begun the therapy."

"Good. The next shipment is next to the door."

Butler walks to it, gets it under his arm, is halfway out the door before White calls after him.

"There is also a device in there. A tracking device, let's say. Its interface should be familiar to you. I believe you will need it."

Then they really think this Katherine hoodrat is hobbling around town, carrying the next step toward their cure in her veins.

It's a relief, yes. It is also a cliff before a long fall, and not many good handholds.

White wishes him a good night, doesn't have to say the rest. Doesn't have to make a threat.

Butler gets in his car and heads for the plasma center. He has to make this up to White, and fast.

43

It's been years since Cora found herself at a house party, and it's older faces here than it was then, though maybe some of the same people. It's a crowded front porch that immediately feels familiar and she was never really a fan. Too humid tonight but they're out in defiance, slouching on secondhand lawn chairs, pretending like they hadn't quit smoking. Like it's ten years ago and they're gonna skip class in the morning.

Cora shifts around on the section of the porch railing she's staked out for a seat. Someone from SpeakScript is talking about whether movies help make people indifferent towards violence. It's not completely clear where he stands, but he sure is using a lot of words to get there. Cora blinks back cigarette smoke and focuses instead on the man to her other side, lanky, wearing a gray tee shirt tightly in the humidity. He rolls his eyes around the patio while a woman in a deck chair across from him talks, then returns to the woman with a smile.

"I don't know, it's nice to be out of the house, is all. You know? People could be talking about whatever and I'd be okay. And anyway, it's not like people are going to see *Die Hard* and then start shooting up their…"

Cora glances through the window into the better-lit living room. Through the empty shelf dividing off the kitchen, she can see only shapes, the color of a passing shirt or a length of forearm, but she doesn't think that any of them are Mitch. He talked her into coming out here with him, saying that a lot of the "old crew" would be there.

Cora's not sure she can remember who exactly that crew involves, or whether she and Mitch would agree on its membership.

But she didn't have any more questions for Mitch, and he didn't know anything else to tell her. To his credit, he proposed a visit to the party at the exact moment that she was done bankrolling his afternoon binge.

Gray Shirt's getting into a story now, stands up. Cora realizes everyone else is listening to him, tries to recognize his face.

"You're telling me she didn't do it?"

"No, man, that's just it." He holds up a thumb-and-finger gun. "I mean, I know what a finger feels like, right? Like, don't ask, but I know. And that was a finger."

"And she...?"

"Yeah! And swear to god, I kept asking her, pressing her about it, and she just flat-out would not admit that she did it."

"What, was it that bad?"

"No! I mean, no. It was fine. Just, I do not get why she was pretending it didn't happen."

Cora gets inside to wrangle Mitch and finds him on the corner of the couch studying some kind of flyer.

"I'm ready to split."

Mitch nods. "Yeah, sure, catch you around."

Never mind her ride back, she supposes.

"Hey, you see these?"

She takes the paper from him, and it's not a band notice, not an apartment ad or a pitch for guitar lessons. The print job's cheap like that, the ink already coming off on her hands, but it's got a medical cross and a cartoon drop of blood with a dollar sign in the middle of it.

"Where's this from?"

"Dunno. They had it taped up over the dishwasher, all ironic-like, but people have been seeing them around. Somebody saw it on campus, somebody else on the telephone pole outside the Wal-Mart. They've been putting them up around SpeakScript faster than they can get torn down. Sticking them next to shitty jobs, I guess."

Cora nods, hands the flyer back. Could be these plasma center people have a better timeline than she does.

THREE

DANI BLINKS HERSELF AWAKE AGAIN, CAN'T TELL where she is. The sunlight is dimmer than the last couple times she woke, but it only feels like a few seconds. Like her heavy eyelids dragged the sun down with them.

The thought of the void she's been slipping into, that she's only broken the surface of to gulp air a couple times, lurks under even these waking moments, more tidal than threatening. She blinks it back, but it spills in through the cracks in her mind and starts to blot everything out. A noise from the side, a stirring, brings her to. The sudden jolt of alertness crawls under her skin but she turns her head and focuses anyway.

The dimming sunlight is bright enough to glint off little crystals in the concrete she's staring at. The curb materializes at eye level through her haze and the noise comes again, a scratching, and it's not coming from a person. It's coming from something like a huge spider, easily as wide as a human torso and nearly as long. Twelve pairs of legs, three on the side nearest her cracked open and hollowed out, faded to an ash grey, dull green streaks around the notches

Katherine's teeth left. They contract slowly, catching and scratching against the grains of the concrete. The sound of drying out, the sound of death.

But this husk doesn't look like anything that could have been alive. Where it's not torn it looks like an obsidian sculpture, smooth and shiny, until what must be the torso shifts, putting its good arms between it and Dani.

She fades again, less completely. Grips the edge of consciousness as her eyes close and open again. Thin green fluid strings from the edges of the torn legs, reaching for the ground. Dani shakes her head to bring herself around. It almost works.

She's swimming in a semi-narcotic haze but she saw the spider before, wrapped around a dead human leg. Only now considers that she's probably cracked her head along the way. But the haze is heavier than that, and the creature is here beside her, getting its good legs under itself and tensing, waiting.

There's something else nearby, besides the shell, the monster. A presence not making noise, but she feels it. Someone familiar. She turns her head and reels and the darkness floods back in again.

Shaking dispels it a little. Back to the margins where it had been. It's still there, but she can see the second figure now, hunched over from the base of the spine, torso and limbs hanging scarecrow-loose. Head cocked but oriented correctly with the ground, how it would be if the figure were standing.

She. If *she* were standing.

Under the dried blood and the dull green crust around her mouth and beneath her nose, Dani recognizes Katherine. Katherine's body, broken to this hanging thing. Clothes hanging loose except where they're fastened to her skin in drying gore, hers and the dead woman's and the creature's. Her face under the residue somewhere. But it's her.

Whatever she thought might have happened to Katherine, it's much worse.

Katherine leers. Muscles slack in the face, slack all around except for what's necessary to keep her standing.

"Katherine. Katherine? My god."

Katherine makes vowel shapes with her mouth, hisses air out. Her lips and her breath not quite connecting, something laryngeal not getting in on the speech.

"I mean. I mean, can you even understand me?"

Katherine nods hard. "Ah. Ah. Yes."

"Where were you?"

"I was hungry. I was so hungry."

Dani tries not to let her eyes dart to the carcass on the curb, but Katherine isn't clocking her face, isn't looking to gauge her reactions. And Dani is only now taking in the empty road they're on the side of, the grass, the sticky air vibrating over the cracked asphalt. They must have walked out here from the storage unit. Katherine must have carried her.

But Katherine says she was hungry. Dani wonders whether that past tense is right.

"Yeah," Dani says. "I noticed."

"I was so hungry." Her mouth works on still air again, searching, getting the feel. "But nothing..."

Dani watches Katherine, but there's no more forthcoming.

She remembers driving to the storage unit. The place isn't in sight in any direction. "We need to go back and get my car."

Katherine stares and runs a finger along the edge of her mouth. She bends at the waist like a badly operated marionette and picks up the vile thing, gathering all its legs, broken and not, into her arms. She cradles it like a child.

WHAT BUTLER HAD HOPED White would hint at was about how the situation had been contained, the problem resolved. A knowing wink or a sidelong smile, but instead White acted like Butler was in charge of cleanup, so now he has to be.

His most promising patient has been at large for nearly two days. He has to clean up after himself, and fast.

The next morning, before work, he drives out to the storage unit he gave Anya the key for. Sun just cresting. Eyes rubbing raw against the sleep he didn't really get. The wheel feels like rubber in his hands and the car floats over the road in that bad-news way that means driving isn't as easy as it's feeling.

But if Anya's still in town she's gone to the storage unit, and if she's there she's a loose end. White made clear who was responsible for the loose ends. Her path out of town got a lot longer with her lackey dead, the premature symbiont clutching bloody holes in her leg. Butler wonders what kind of scene he might be driving toward.

Hopefully she's there. Butler would rather clean up bodies than hunt.

The storage facility comes up and the lot is empty as always. He does three laps around the place, up and down each of the four rows, before he's satisfied that no one is there, no one is waiting for him. Still parks a few units down.

He tries his key on two wrong locks. He's only ever been here the once, to put eighteen months down on the unit. The third lock, though, he knows it's the right one from the smell.

It's a moldy, coppery scent that sticks in the back of his throat and brings thin bile up to meet it. He throws the door to the unit open before he can think better of it. The air in the unit rushes outside, as repulsed as he is, and Butler's eyes only half adjust to the interior dimness before something primal kicks over and he turns away from the doorway and spits up the breakfast he didn't have in tortuous mucousy strands.

The blood runs up the walls, long arcing streaks. Not from puncture wounds and ruptured arteries but thrashing about wounded. Thin splashes, already drying at their peaks.

The rest is pooled in a smeared puddle against one wall. Footprints and handprints and the shapes of Rorschach dreams. Butler spends his days handling the stuff, drawing it and filtering out part of it and storing that part in neat vials, pumping the rest, with or without White's experimental additive, back into the body. But he so rarely sees it in this uncontrolled form, spilling and spreading outside of the neat confines of its usual glass tubes.

Laboratory blood has no such impulse to chaos, to suggestion.

Butler tracks the shapes in the blood, looks for any story at all. Doesn't find one on offer. Overlapping trails and smears, too much activity for the one body in evidence.

Butler swallows hard and steps toward the body. He keeps his sneakers as far from the blood as possible, for as long as possible, tiptoeing in the gaps between this splash, that smear. But a couple feet from the body the spatter stops and the pool begins.

He flattens his feet, presses against the wall. Leans down from the waist, trembling, not willing to brace himself on the floor, get the blood on his hands.

It's already on his shoes. That's plenty.

He pulls a pen from his pocket, pokes it forward to lift the body's hair. The brutal smell hovers in a cloud here. Butler finds himself holding his breath. All he has to do is confirm that that the body is Katherine's and he can leave.

He gets the tip of the pen under some of the hair and knows it's not Katherine's. Too short. He peels the rest of the hair from the skin and looks down at the bruise-bloated face of Anja, the postmortem sneer her lips are already pulling into.

It should be a relief. But Butler remembers the pincers dug into her leg, fleeing the hotel. This specimen is the earliest to be removed from its host, the only one not delivered to a controlled Institute environment, and it seems to have been viable. The new dosage might be to blame, or something he didn't know to look for in the blood work. Either way, Anja couldn't have removed the thing from her leg alone, without tools.

However it happened, the symbiont is *gone*. Not dead in the corner or clinging to Anja's leg but removed by someone who was able to close and lock the door behind them.

Perhaps it was the patient. Katherine. He looks up to the top of the doorway, maybe eight feet high, and tries to imagine her reaching that high in the shape he last saw her.

It's impossible, but so is all of this. Better to focus on what's in front of him, see where that leads.

He sticks the pen under her pant leg. The denim clings

a bit at first, then squelches free. Skin like dog-eaten tissue paper, residue of the specimen's green blood. Some other substance, too, black as the creature's embryotic fluid but without the glimmer.

Butler stares awhile. Can't figure out what that could be.

They need more tests, more patients.

He braves the blood to slide his hand into Anja's hip pocket. The envelope is there, sticky and damp. He pulls out the cash and drops the envelope back on the body. Finds a blue surgical glove in his own pocket, stuffs the money inside and ties off the wrist. Wishes he'd found the glove before touching Anja.

He steps back carefully, trying to keep his toes in the footprints he's already left. Nearly to the edge of the pool he gets careless, lets his foot hit the ground flat. Traction gives like a carnival ride and he pitches backward into the puddle.

His control fails. He jerks and writhes and pulls himself toward the door, looking back at the smearing trail he's left, the blood angel where he fell. It covers his footprints but his clothes are ruined.

And the unit is in his name. For the moment that's safe enough, but eventually insects and scavengers will follow their noses and bring attention trailing after, even here.

Time was, Anja'd be the first person he'd think to call in a situation like this.

Now he'll have to call White again, for another Institute clean-up.

He strips down to undershirt and shorts, rolls his clothes into a ball and tucks them under his arm. Heaves the door up and slams it down behind him and forces the lock closed and takes off toward his car in a crouching run before his eyes have adjusted at all.

FLASHES, at first. Disjointed memories. Snapshots and phantom sensations. The pressure plays on Katherine's skin for real, memories triggering nerves and interrupting her actual interaction with the motel room around her.

Something is happening, but she can't keep hold of where it is. Or where she is.

She knows her name from what Dani calls her. Katherine.

She feels hot then less hot, feels something growing inside her and tearing out before it's done and the impossible problem of reintroducing it after the fact. Increasingly certain this is a memory.

Chewing on flesh that tastes like her own. Crunching through the hard shell into also hard but wet alien flesh and the swallowing coming easier than she'd expected, scratching the hunger itch that none of the scraps of human skin in her teeth could.

But it helped some, helped her discover a bit of the person Dani still thinks she is.

And now she can barely stand to put the thing down.

Dani sleeps, finally. Katherine's been waiting for that since they came upon the motel near sunrise and Dani gathered herself enough to go in alone and come out with a key. It took until the day was getting dark again. She lets her creature walk around the little room. She can smell the man next door. He's not sleeping, growing more agitated and trying hard to keep a lid on it. It's all in the way he's sweating. It's something like smelling a taste, a body-language cue.

Whatever she is, she doesn't think she's quite Katherine anymore.

The room around her nearly floats. Now in sync with how she feels it, now blurring radically out of phase. But the shadows and the furniture and Dani's flopped-sideways figure solidify and stay.

Katherine fixes her eyes on Dani, mouths her name, then her own. Tries to get her mouth used to the shapes. Dani has stopped flinching when Katherine speaks except when she says either of their names.

Her creature crawls along the wall behind the bed where Dani sleeps. Katherine sits on the single chair in the room, in a way that Dani clearly found hard to look at. She hasn't moved for hours, remembers vaguely that she would have found that impossible a week or two ago. The creature paces back and forth, like on a rail along that wall. The strong legs scrape loudly when they're against the wall. The cleaned-out legs whisper like paper.

The man in that room might have seen them through his window, but she doesn't think it matters. She stays tuned anyway to all the sounds in the room, whether they originate there or not. Tracking, remembering. She remembers so little that now she's trying to register everything.

FOUR

THE AIR CONDITIONING IS ICY IN THE PLASMA CLINIC, the room surprisingly bright behind the charcoal-gray privacy glass. The door doesn't make a sound closing behind her, and a woman at a little desk to Cora's right nods about as friendly as a brick wall. There's one man sitting in one of a row of what look like ratty dentist's chairs, tourniquet loose around his arm. Waiting.

The doctor will be in soon, sure.

The woman pushes a clipboard across the desk, doesn't notice how Cora's not reaching for it. "You have to fill this out. If you've gotten a tattoo or traveled outside the country or had homosexual relations in the last—"

"I don't think I need to—"

"We're not hiring."

Cora shakes her head, tugs the collar tighter on the orange-and-pink windbreaker Katherine didn't pack to take with her, because she didn't take anything. "No, I mean I've been here before."

The woman looks her over like maybe she looks familiar. Maybe.

"All right. Driver's license?"

"What? I left it at home," scanning the woman's shirt for a nametag, barely finding it hung jauntily from an open buttonhole, nearly illegible for all the no one who'd care to look for it, "Janet. Come on, don't you recognize me."

Janet's face switches off and she pulls the clipboard back. "Nope, sorry. Come back with your license."

"For fucksake, I work...I mean, come on, isn't the doctor here?"

"The *technician* is in the back right now. But that doesn't change anything."

"You've got my name in there somewhere, right?" Gesturing at the several stacked desktop organizers full of file folders. "Katherine Suwalksi."

Janet's eyes track down to a folder on top of a little stack on her desk, like she remembers it's there, and Cora sees Katherine's name in sharpie on a stick-on label before Janet sweeps the stack even, hides the label.

They both stare at the stack. Cora tries to weigh whether she's better served pushing or looking desperate.

Janet breaks the silence. "New haircut or something? I'm sure I don't recognize you."

The door in back of the room opens and gives Cora a second. A frazzled-looking man emerges, rubbing his washed-raw hands with a wad of paper towels. His face catches the light dully, like he's wearing foundation he almost knows how to apply. He shoves the towels into a trash can and walks to the donor in the chair. Tightens the tourniquet before speaking too low for Cora to hear.

Janet calls over to him, but he waves her off. Janet sighs and closes her eyes over everything she's not saying, and Cora warms not inconsiderably to the clerk.

"Well, whatever. Katherine, you said?"

"Suwalksi, yeah."

Janes rifles through the sheaf of folders, fingers fast and precise against her general laconic manner. She pinpoints the right one and flips it open. Cora tries to imitate Katherine's signature as best she can, and gets pretty close, but Janet doesn't look at it, just waves her into the main room, toward a chair.

Cora listens as she walks, worried there's some part of the procedure she doesn't know about, like whether she's supposed to wait until she's offered a chair or something. Nobody lifts their heads when she sits, though, across the aisle from the man with the tourniquet and as close to the back as possible.

She slides down a little in the chair, trying to find something that feels like how Katherine would sit. The slumping feels wrong but she leans into it, shaking her hair down over her face and hoping the jacket does some of the work.

She had assumed the place would be busier than this. Maybe this is the wrong time. There's no crowd to disappear into, though, no wait. Cora starts to form questions. There's a limit on the number of times a person can sell a month, she thinks she remembers, so she can probably get the last time Katherine was here out of the needle man. She's not sure where to go from there, had somehow not figured she might have to let them punch needles through her skin.

But the tech comes back through the back door, glancing at her through the side of his eyes. Cora relaxes a bit until the guy pulls his hands out of lab-coat pockets to take the clipboard and does a double-take back to her, to the name on the sign-in, to the way Cora's hair isn't even that close to Katherine's.

"That's some jacket," he says, thumbing a phone up from his back pocket.

And Cora's off, hitting the back door with her wrists before anyone else moves, bursting into a back office, smaller than she'd imagined but with a door leading further back, out the rear wall of the strip mall. She smiles, presses her back to the door she came through. Takes a minute to get her bearings.

Boxes and shelves full of shrink-wrapped stuff, plastic tarps over little piles of things that don't look much used. A black metal workbench off in the corner, dust-free and with a little overhead light going.

Several boxes of needles and ampules to one side, little drawer of orange-tape-wrapped ones open on the other side of the desk.

Like someone doesn't want to get them crossed.

Something seems fucking rotten in the plasma kingdom.

A weight slams against the door and into her back, harder than she'd expected but she keeps it closed. Spots a wallet on the bench next to the needles and plots a route, snags the wallet on the way to the back door.

Crashes hard into reinforced metal. Spies as she's hitting the ground the gleaming new lock drilled in above an old peeling knob. Her wrists scream and feel spongy, compressed. Her vision blurs over the sickening suspicion that she might have broken her arms, here.

The door to the main room clangs open and the needle man stomps in.

Cora groans her way back up to her feet, trying to feel her arms as she pushes against the spotless floor. The man doesn't really block the door, just strolls in hands-on-hips like this is a scam for needles, and Cora sees the only window she's going to get and runs. The man realizes his mistake a hand's length too late and Cora's past his reach and through the front room and into the sunlight.

It might not matter but she reaches back to ruck the hood of Katherine's jacket up over her head, against the security cameras. If they have them inside the plasma center they'll have a clear photo in an hour or two, but Cora has the feeling that maybe the inside is a dead zone, that maybe they're only looking to record who comes in and out, not what they're doing inside.

She gets around the corner and down a street. Cheap houses with overly cared-for flowering bushes. The flowers will last all year. She ducks between two houses and onto an even smaller street and finally pulls the wallet from her pocket, kicking herself for bailing with nothing more than that. This was her chance, after all, and that back room had plenty she would have been interested in. It might not even be the right wallet.

The driver's license is a familiar face, though, minus about an elbow's worth of bruising and a couple of years. The security photo in the corner of the credit card, a feature Cora's never seen before, has the same face.

Johannes Butler. She reads it twice and almost smiles.

CORA'S CALL is quick and hard. Mitch tries to tell her he doesn't want to get involved, doesn't know anything about anything and is sorry if he freaked her out, but it's like talking to a recording.

She repeats the name, says he needs to go check on the guy. It sounds like someone who discovered something, an atomic particle or maybe a planet. Certainly no one named Johannes is walking around still, not in this hemisphere.

He tries to tell Cora that, too. She is not bursting with curiosity or courtesy on the matter.

"All right, but you owe me one," he tells the going-dead line. Cora probably doesn't see it that way.

And that's the deal with getting involved. He's felt it enough times.

Plus, he's still a little high from lunch.

Cora said she's midtown without her car. So maybe he'll just look up the guy's address and call that back to her. His laptop's on his lap anyway. What the hell.

It's no big trick to find him. The name's distinctive and he has his medical qualifications. It takes a little while to get a residential location, though; most of what Mitch finds are professional listings, the registration for the plasma center, assorted documentation. One licensing site finally leads him to a spreadsheet with a posted address.

He picks up the phone to call Cora, but there isn't really any way to make sure that the listed address is still valid. And he's started to invest in the task a little bit.

It's momentum. Poke your head into something and it gets stuck, drags you along behind it.

He gets up off the couch. The world doesn't spin so much as get a little fuzzy for a moment. The edges come back, though, and things stabilize when he steps out into the driveway and gives himself a moment to adjust to the light and climbs into the driver's seat.

He smiles, letting the moment get to his head a little bit. Here comes ol' Mitch, bumbling straight on through to the rescue.

The address is hard to find. Johannes lives way south. Mitch always thinks of Miller Road as the end of town, forgetting that across from the ring of big-box stores and chain restaurants is a whole nest of houses too big for him to think about, hidden behind a little green belt and the frontage road.

Mitch doesn't even know the names of these roads, is operating on the vague memory of the computer map back home. The grid that shakily holds the rest of the town together melts down here. Miller Road does a lazy arc toward the highway and the roads coming off it swirl around in its wake. Mitch turns off into a neighborhood that might be correct and tries to navigate it like doing a maze with your finger: always turning right.

The street he's looking for comes up somehow on the left while he's doubling back. Mitch gasps when he sees the sign, a little shocked that his maze routine didn't pay off, but when he gets a look at the street and sees that it's barely more than a notch in the side of a different street, three houses and a fourth on the corner, he feels a little better.

This neighborhood is a different world from where he lives. It must be seventy percent lawns.

He parks as near the little blip of a road as he can, so he has a view of all the mailboxes. The one he's after is in the middle of three. He double-checks the address.

It's right, and he wonders what exactly Katherine had gotten herself into. It's a cookie-cutter suburb house, sure, but one of the massive farm-looking ones, roof dipping down a little over the front and the bulk of the house behind it making the awning look like an undersized hat. The architectural equivalent of an overstuffed bag of produce. Mitch imagines a caving-outward of drywall, an avalanche of two-by-fours and insulation and glass.

Cora thinks the guy who lives in that monstrosity might have something to do with Katherine's disappearance. What would that kind of money even be interested in someone like Katherine for?

Stick your nose in, see where you get dragged.

The garage door opens. Mitch slides lower in the seat, kills the engine. A short man, clean-cut in a white jacket and sneakers, scrambles across to the single Volvo in the middle. He looks over his shoulders though he hasn't gotten outside yet. Pats down his jacket pockets until he finds keys and gets in the car.

Mitch follows him at a distance. The heavy traffic on Miller makes it easier not to get caught but harder to keep this Butler character in sight, and kicks up the remnants of his afternoon smoke into an edginess he hasn't felt in a long time.

It has to be Butler. The coincidence of Cora's call and this hasty exit is too much for otherwise.

Mitch would sure feel a lot more confident if he knew where Butler was leading him to.

At first it seems like the university, the way he darts into the left lane. But then Butler changes again and Mitch has to cut someone off. Butler eases up on the gas a little through sorority row and past some student apartments, then picks it up again when he crosses from the college periphery into a one-slumlord neighborhood, takes a residential road up past the boarded-up south end of Main Street and out onto where downtown starts.

Mitch frowns, looks around like he's missed something. There's nowhere this is the fastest way to get to. No traffic being avoided. It's like Butler's trying to make the drive as difficult as possible for himself.

Mitch lets his foot off the pedal, coasts until someone pulls between him and Butler.

Mitch braces for some quick turn, some jag into an

alley. Decides that when it comes, the evasion that will confirm Mitch has been spotted, he's going to give up the game, get on the phone to Cora and tell her where Butler was last seen.

It doesn't come, though.

Mitch figures this means the guy's paranoid but not very good at what he's trying to do. He understands that feeling.

Now that they've broken through the worst of the congestion, Mitch ferrets his phone up through an uncooperative jeans pocket and dials Cora. Pins the tinny speaker to his ear with his shoulder.

"Yeah."

"North on East 15th."

"When? Now?"

"Yeah, I—"

"You were supposed to call if he left."

"Yeah, I mean, he left pretty fast."

"North on Southeast 15th."

"Um. No, Northeast 15th."

Cora does frustrated blast of sigh-static and hangs up. Mitch flicks the turn signal for an eventual U-turn out of this situation, lets it click. Flicks it back off again.

Tells himself he ought to go home. Bail on this whole freaky shit-parade and let the maelstrom consume itself. It's not like he owes Cora any favors.

No, but he does owe Katherine a couple, if she ever cared to count them.

He twists his hands on the wheel and follows Butler out of the town proper and into the county, toward the swamp and the complicated streams and an abandoned bait shop.

CORA FOLLOWS Mitch's directions to the hiss-whispered letter, nearly misses the turnoff to the bait shop's drive anyway. It's a dirt road off a gravel one, trees all around, a little glimmer of the lake through one side. Already dark though it's barely past sunset. The sign in front just says *bait*, probably has since before Cora was born. A little cluster of holes from a bored shotgun.

She backs up and parks a little ways away in the woods and circles back, keeping to the trees until she sees Mitch crouched, waving her over and to keep down. She nods, no kidding, and sidles up next to him.

He points to the cabin. "What are you going to say to him?"

She shrugs. "Sure he's in there?"

"Yeah. Watch."

They stare at the lit window and hold their breath. Cora thinks she sees the shadow of a man pass one instant, second-guesses that the next.

"Alone?"

Mitch gestures to where they are. "No other cars. He's just pacing around. What are you going to say?"

Cora touches the pocketknife in her pocket. It feels smaller and lighter, less formidable, than it did an hour ago. "I'll figure it out. No way out of there?"

"Unless he has himself a boat."

They both look toward the lake, the rotting dock collapsed into the water.

"If he's waiting, most likely he's waiting for someone,

right?" Cora says. "Let's get in there before they do."

"What do you mean *let's*?"

She stares at him as hard as she can but he doesn't flinch, just waits with his eyebrows up.

"Hang back here, okay?" she says. "Give me fifteen minutes and call the cops, then get out."

"I'll call the cops from down the road."

Cora claps him on the shoulder and sets off in a crab-walk toward the building. The light coming through the window is dim enough that if she stares at it too long it fades. She presses her face to the edge of the window.

It's Butler in there, for sure. He's kept the white coat on, has a large leather case and a rolling suitcase with him. He paces around the dusty wares of a long-dead business, from the shelf to the counter and back. The leather case is on a card table in the middle of the room, a little bubble of the present.

He freezes and peers at the opposite window. Cora smiles. Wrong one, asshole. He shakes his head, visibly reassuring himself that it's the wind, that no one knows he's here.

Cora finds to her surprise that her hands aren't shaking, but the breath she pulls to ready herself comes much shallower than she expects, like she's having to pull it through a very narrow opening indeed.

She crawls around the corner and eases the screen door open slowly, wary of rust and squeaking springs, but it pulls smooth, has had its closing mechanism disconnected.

The front door is unlocked.

Butler reaches the shelf and pauses an extra second. Hand to his head. He shakes whatever off and paces back toward the counter.

Cora kicks the front door as hard as she can, but it's all

damp wood and plaster so she doesn't get the jarring clang she's after, just a soft thunk.

Butler still jumps and spins and almost rolls his ankle in the process

Cora lets the door bounce back closed behind her.

"What in the world are you doing here?"

"I'm looking for someone."

"They're not here."

"You don't want to know who?"

"There is no one else here."

"You know who. You recognized her jacket and panicked and now here we are."

Cora raises the blade to eye level. Butler shrugs.

Cora covers the room in three long strides but Butler's not where he was a second ago. Hands slap her between the shoulder blades and it's enough to turn her run into a sprawl. Yellow linoleum comes up hard. The knife bites into her skin where her hand chokes up, but she doesn't let go. Roll over and scrambles to a crouch.

The adrenaline's going, but it's pushing a worry along with it, that the wide-eyed man across from her is the wrong guy, that he doesn't know what's happened to her girlfriend, that this is going to become that kind of news story.

Florida Woman Stabs Doctor in Shed. Lovelorn Lesbian Murders Real Citizen.

But then Butler's face hardens and he smiles a little. "If I were you, I would leave before I got answers."

Cora lunges for him again. Keeps her center of gravity low this time, her eyes on Butler's leg. The pocketknife wouldn't be much use for slashing, but she sticks it into his hip. Thin skin like taut paper and bone like rock. She drags the blade, rends more skin.

Butler shouts. She wiggles the slick blade out from

between her fingers and grips the handle. Butler stumbles against the wall and onto his knees.

Cora is startled by the bone-deep urge to keep cutting. To never stop cutting. It's better to have something to cut than only an absence to deal with.

She comes in hard and low, bringing the knife around. Butler raises his arm over his throat and rolls, takes the point of the blade glancingly off his shoulder blade. He kicks Cora's legs back from under her and she falls onto him fore-arm-first, just below his ribcage.

Butler's breath rushes out. Cora climbs up his torso. His eyes go wide. Some kind of noise from outside, a rustling, that she registers absently and raises the knife, hovers its point over one dilating pupil, preparing a question meant to be final, one way or the other.

And the front door bursts open.

THE GIRL HAS Butler bleeding on the floor. White lets the security people stabilize that before he takes a second step inside the meeting place. He has a half-dozen with him, two more in the van. The entry team takes the girl by the shoulders, rams her clear against the opposite wall, and hauls Butler to his feet only a bit gentler.

The advantages to his position aren't surprising to him anymore, but they still do feel nice. Nothing smooths out volatile moments like well-armed security.

"We have a situation," Butler says, trying to come toward White but impeded by kevlar arms.

White lets Butler watch him awhile. Butler's got his

sycophant face going, appealing to a sense of loyalty he thinks White values.

"S*ituation* is one way to put it."

The girl strikes while White's head is turned. A guard drops to the ground, holding his bottom rib, where the armor doesn't cover. Two more take her down hard, and White winces for a second until some profanity confirms she's still conscious.

"Who's your new friend?"

"She came in just a minute before you did."

White sighs. Points to the guard nearest the door, then out the door. The man nods, takes another with him for cover. He had seen the second car in the woods and assumed that Butler had felt nervous enough to bring some muscle along.

Butler watches them leave, face slack with incomprehension. White holds his eyes a little while. Smiles a little bit and turns to the girl.

"Now, I don't believe we've met."

The prisoner thrashes against the two guards holding her. Blood trickling from somewhere on her lips, her forehead. Flashing teeth shadowed in gummy blood.

She's halfway up despite the two very large men hired precisely for their ability to keep someone pinned down. White considers her. Most likely she doesn't know much of anything. Even so, here she is, in a location no one is supposed to stumble into.

And she does seem strong. The Institute does not lack for funding but has, with Butler's help, recently come into a more urgent need for trial subjects.

One of the guards jerks her up, holds her face toward White. Waiting.

White waves at the door the door. "Let's take a ride,

shall we?"

One of the guards pulls a zip tie from his belt and secures her wrists. White turns to Butler, who's getting the same treatment. White waves the guards off, cuts the ties from Butler's wrist.

Butler's proven himself dangerous, of course, a definite liability, but he might be salvageable.

"Apologies," he says while Butler rubs his wrists. "You know they're trained to keep a situation under control."

"Okay, but they should know whose side I'm on. You should know."

White does. Butler is a true believer.

"Butler, when they're called in, it's because there's a crisis. They treat every engagement like a crisis engagement."

Butler's been a wonderful contractor, nearly untraceable to the Institute and completely committed to his mission, but there's nothing more dangerous than a crusader. Like a chess piece that feels strongly about which squares it's willing to land on, a risk to go rogue if the specifics of the project don't line up with what they've imagined.

The choices are to cut him loose and protect the Institute, or bring him in closer and see which way he breaks.

"Come with us. We have some things that we need to discuss."

Butler nods seriously and follows him outside, flicking off the light behind him. The guards have wrangled their prisoner into to the back of one of the black vans and stand around it, keeping watch. White holds the door of the other for Butler and they pile in. The other van pulls out first.

They cruise through nighttime streets, skirting the bright lights still burning downtown and turning toward campus, keeping to the shadows but not hiding. White can feel Butler's eyes on him, tries to mimic the expression he'd wear if this were a routine debrief, if Butler were a trusted colleague.

Nearly to the Institute, White chances a look at him. He's looking out the window, tracking the passing streets and buildings like he hadn't already memorized them. He reads calm, which tells White nothing in particular.

The lead van's driver swipes his ID card at the campus hospital back gate. His card isn't enough clearance for two vehicles, so White's van has to stop at the booth for White to swipe them through. The gate buzzes open and the vans pull into the hospital lot, weaving past the main building to the lot of the smaller structure housing the main laboratory entrance.

White opens his door and walks a purposeful dozen yards away to watch the crew unload the girl.

He should learn her name, he supposes, though the circumstances will eliminate most of the usual perfunctory niceties of paperwork. The internal records will still have to be kept.

Two guards pull her headfirst and facedown from the van. One holds her dangling head and shoulders below the running board so she's hanging half in the van. The other guard works a two-bandana system over her head, one wrapped around her skull, the other balled and filling her mouth, and ties it tight. He's quick about it, but it takes his hands off her momentarily. She bends her whole back behind a heel kick, flips right over the other guard's hands on her shoulders.

She hangs in the air an impossible moment, just long enough for White to note how there's no one between her and the road past the building.

She rides the arc of her kick all the way around, until her feet stall out pointing straight up. She hits the concrete with the back of her head and her shoulders.

Six guards swoop in while she's dazed, the two who lost her trying to redeem themselves with diving elbows to her head and ribs.

White hasn't moved. Her persistence is pleasant.

The guards hustle her upright, if limp and moaning, precise in the way a grunt gets when a supervisor is watching.

White leads them to the door and punches in the night-time code. One of the drivers pulls the heavy door open when the lock beeps. White strides into his home base of gleaming linoleum and fluorescent lights.

There is no front desk, no receptionist. This is not a place for visitors. No appointments with the outside are made or kept. The Institute uses a small office in the administrative wing of the hospital for what few meetings are required and doesn't grant interviews to the press. An occasional reporter or student or job-seeker will try to schedule one, and find themselves rerouted through a series of dummy offices. If they're persistent enough, they might get on the line a person at an unwitting subsidiary of the Institute under instructions to inform them that this building is leased to a private partner of the university for practical research and development, and to hint there might be national security implications.

One guard slips ahead and comes back with a gurney. He is well-trained and quiet. The Institute does not use the university's security personnel in here. The girl looks dazed from her fall, isn't fighting the arms forcing her onto the gurney.

"You may have sustained some injuries in your fall,"

White says. "This is an unfortunate development; you were reckless. You'll find, though, that even though our Institute," he hopes she can hear the capital *I*, "is in no way responsible for such injuries, since we do after all have the right to protect our business ventures, we will nonetheless furnish treatment that will, I assure you, address whatever physical damage you may have incurred."

She stares up at him. Blood smeared around her broken nose. Left eye folding into a flower of bruised flesh. Her mouth works silently.

It's a shame. Her new role as a patient was made so much more interesting by her anger, her fortitude. Perhaps she hurt herself more than it appeared. In a few hours they'll know for sure. By then, as long as nothing immanently fatal has burst internally, it likely won't matter much.

White points to her pocket. One of the guards extracts a wallet. White flips it open, reads:

"Cora Bruno." He peeks over the top of the license, meets her wide eyes. "I do hope you enjoy your stay."

CORA'S EYES creep open on a harsh white light. Rude intrusive feeling in her arms. Maybe needles. Shapes of people, gleaming white bodies and hands and upper faces, indistinct everywhere else. She stares until it makes sense: surgical masks and protective gloves, white rubber coats.

Thoughts come slowly, don't respond to what she's seeing until the scene has shifted. Constant game of catch-up.

Her head hit the parking lot. That would be the source

of some of the drowsiness, but not all of it. The tubes snaking through the margins of her vision must account for the rest.

If only she could see where they were entering her body, somehow it would be easier to bear.

One face dips lower than the others. Wide steel eyes, high forehead. Amiable expression spread thin over something much harder. The leader from the bait shop, the man in the suit.

He's holding a needle, and this is when Cora discovers the thick leather straps around her waist and ankles and wrists. They dig into her skin long seconds before she registers the pain, and by then all that's left of White and the needle is a burning in her arm that spreads through her veins like hot metal.

From the back of the room: "It's important that you be awake for this part, you understand."

White, again. So he hasn't disappeared.

"We have to be able to gauge your reaction. Your physical state. We have to be able to see your facial expressions." Friendly like a concierge. "We can't have you sedated, for this part of the therapy."

The molten steel in her veins rolls Cora's eyes back into her head.

"Remember, we are here to treat you. To cure what ails."

A sound like a speaker clicking off and Cora wonders whether the man was ever in the room with her at all as the shadows creep in from the corners.

The darkness she slips into isn't empty.

There are voices. Floating at a distance, reaching Cora as through a layer of cotton. Consonants twisting around themselves, vowelless. Inflections beyond any spoken accent but still achingly familiar.

But she can't feel her body.

That's not quite right. There are feelings, but they're registering as a second set of sounds, humming under the voices. They drone for an eternity, the sole focus of her attention, and start to take on meanings.

Not meanings. Origins.

This buzz spreads from the impact zone the asphalt left in the top of her head, that hum from the punctures of heavy-gauge needles through her skin. The rhythms of heavy dehydration and adrenaline hangover, saline drip and sedative unconsciousness fight it out in something like a physical discordant harmony, testing each other's borders, pushing against each other.

It's all on the skin, the eardrums, whatever new organ is sensing these vibrations.

Cora familiarizes herself with these secondary sounds, these undergirding sense-melodies. They turn not into vibrations or physical stimulus, but one implying the other. The way a chord implies an emotion.

The decoding stops being decoding and becomes instead a simultaneous dual reception.

And so the voices return to the fore.

They still feel foreign and familiar. The inflections don't correspond to the emotions the voices are carrying.

Their syllables become more similar, drawing closer together in intonation and articulation and begin to chant. The guttural and the sibilant lockstepping into a not-quite-sound. She peers around, tries to twist her head to see, and only then realizes that she can't. Can't see and can't feel, only these weird impressions beyond any sensory organs.

A long way below her, she senses something. Something familiar, warm, changing.

Her own body.

FIVE

MITCH PEELS HIS BOOTS AND SOCKS OFF. ALL THAT fucking mud, soaked up to his ankles and in great kinetic streaks up to his knees. He can feel the contusions rising on his face from tree branches in the dark, mosquito bites scratched to bloody on his arms and neck to stop their itching.

He hates the woods.

He left his car. Probably those cops took it, or had someone watching, but he struck out in the same direction as the cops took Cora and managed to walk home in an hour and change.

The scratchy couch never felt better, but he notices the mud on his legs a second after he flops down. Lifts his hips and peels his jeans down, throws them in the direction of his bedroom.

The liquor stores on the way were all closed so he settles for a tightly packed bowl of shake and a half-fifth of his roommate's Mad Dog from the fridge. Holds the smoke dramatically, like a teenager, and blasts it out in one big cloud to slug down the blue-raspberry wine in one go. One more hit to scratch the itch in his lungs and Mitch turns on the television and drowses in the light of staged pawn-shoppers and historical reenactments.

Let Cora deal with getting herself out of jail. He's done enough for the day. A twinge of guilt so he turns up the TV.

But tires scratch at the gravel driveway and his high goes sideways, the pleasant fuzz laid over the world growing sharp red spines, but he can't quite jump off the couch to flee.

He angles his head down to see under the blinds. Sees a car pulled up, rust spots starting to show through the teal on the bumper.

The car door slams.

Mitch eases to his feet just ahead of the dangerous wobbling the world's trying out. A purple bong is the closest thing to a weapon in the living room, so he hefts it. Tries a couple grips, settles on clutching just above the bottom, thumb near the bowl, long glass pipe snug against his forearm.

Footsteps coming closer. Mitch runs beside the door, sees the deadbolt isn't thrown.

The roommate would be furious.

A knock comes, fast and hard. Somebody's in a hurry. Mitch presses himself against the wall through the second knock, the third, until the doorknob turns and the door's flung open and he raises his weapon above his head.

The bowl slides out, clatters on the floorboards. Cloud of bitter ash swirling around his head, dusting his face. He coughs and swings, slinging a reeking arc of bongwater against the wall. The blow gets stopped before it can land. The intruder shoves his hand back. The rest of him carries with it, stumbles and crashes to the ground.

The bong hangs in the air and the center of his vision,

shatters behind him in a tragic burst. Dust of glass shards and water droplets against the back of his neck.

Mitch scoots back on the floor with his feet until the weed-dust clears enough that he sees Dani's face through it and relaxes a bit.

She doesn't. Steps forward, ready to strike down at him.

He gets his arms up in front of his face. Only now sees the friend lurking behind Dani, clutching a hooded-sweat-shirt bindle. The package squirms against her grip, or else Mitch is higher than he thought.

Dani takes a step back, raises both hands to show how much she's not hitting him right now. "The *fuck*, Mitch?"

"I didn't ... I didn't know. What the hell, you don't call?"

He jumps up, lets the living room smear around him, and as it's re-congealing and Dani sneers at him, the friend tilts her head up enough for Mitch to make her out through the greased-down hair and heavily bagged eyes.

Katherine.

He leaps past Dani's rising guard and throws his arms around Katherine, pulls her to him. Her neck carries her head away from him even as her body moves closer. The bundle rustles faster.

Sharp brief pain in his midsection. He sees a gleaming knobbed arm pull itself back into its cotton wrapping.

The sweatshirt has surfboards and a smiling cartoon sun, like from a truck-stop gift shop.

His palm comes up a little bloody. Not much. It's a warning stab, maybe.

Katherine angles her body past him and slips into Mitch's roommate's room. No telling, really, when he'll be home. It depends on his schedule this afternoon. Mitch isn't great at keeping track of what days mean what lately.

And the blood trickles down his torso.

Dani winces forward like she's trying to calm him, keep him from screaming, maybe, but that's not what he's feeling. He passes his hands down along his stomach, trailing sticky blood everywhere. His skin gets warm, wet. The high curdling under the adrenaline, and he's pressing down all over himself and wiping down where there's nothing to wipe.

But there's a new feeling, only making him panic more. He feels like he's covered in blood.

Dani touches his face. He freezes, stares at her.

Whatever Katherine's holding had more than just the one leg, moving under the fabric. He must be seeing things, must be high, must be letting the sleepless night and the surprise of his visitors melt reality around him to fit the form of his mind.

Dani grows concerned and blurry. Mitch slumps into her, and she helps him to the couch. He lets her ease him down, the strange sensations already fading, drifting off and leaving him just regular exhausted again.

THE ONE CALLED Dani and the one called Mitch drift around the kitchen. Katherine is getting better at recognizing the figures standing up straight and speaking syllables her brain struggles to synthesize.

Her name is starting to feel right, but the concept isn't. The boundary between the limit of her skin and the air seems too fluid, makes names seem something more of convenience than definition.

Dani is looking worriedly at Mitch, trying to convince

him to sit down or stand still, inching closer to letting her frustration out on him. The smell coming off Mitch is tense, like a second skin pulled tighter over the first.

"This doesn't make any sense," Mitch says.

"What did you expect?"

"I didn't *expect* that I would ever fucking see you again. I thought that you were dead."   "Because of Cora."

"Because you were *gone*. You were gone right after Katherine."

Their heads tilt over towards her. She meets their gaze. They nod to her, comforting, and confirm Katherine's suspicion that they haven't quite noticed that she's not as baffled as that first day, in the storage unit, the door sliding open through the infinite dark like the birth of the first sun.

In any case, they keep talking, not expecting anything from her.

"You have to understand that I wouldn't have gotten myself into this except I wanted to help Katherine."

Dani sighs. "Yeah, I know. You and Katherine."

Neither says anything for a very long time.

Mitch slouches back against the sink. Katherine's getting better at body language, but this one's tough. There's something happening between them that feels old. They don't talk about it but are both thinking of it.

It seems to be about her. Her, and someone called Cora. She might once have known a Cora.

Verbal communication as a wave of noise, carrying driftwood signal along in the foam. Listening for blips in the current. For absence.

"Okay," Mitch says. "All right. I'll help." He looks over to Katherine, then back to Dani. "But not for you."

Dani says very quietly: "One day, you're going to tell me what it is you think you owe her."

A little while later Dani and Mitch are back in the living room. Katherine's still leaning against the far wall, a strange prickling coming over her feet that she remembers. She's trying to figure out what it means, what she would have done about it in the past. No one's talking right now and it doesn't help her think. Silence is too loud, somehow. It helps to hear other people say words but they don't seem to want to right now.

Dani finally breaks. "Mitch, what's going on?"

"What's going on? I mean, you and Katherine, who's been missing for I don't even know—"

"No. Mitch, come on. That's not it. What's going on?"

And something turns over for Katherine. The feeling in her feet. She hauls herself upright off the counter and sets one foot in front of the other. It works. The living room moves past her until she's at the chair no one's using. She smiles and settles down into the chair. Feeling flushes back into her feet. She twists herself around in the seat until it feels right.

Looks up to two pairs of wide eyes staring at her.

It's something to do with how she's sitting, but she's comfortable.

Mitch gets up and walks to the kitchen, starts to pace. Runs one hand along the edge of the sink like he's trying to figure out what it's made of. Frowns and wipes his fingers on his pants.

Something about this makes Dani smell like she misses him.

"Look, it's about Cora," Mitch whispers.

Dani looks over at Katherine again.

"She called me up, trying to call in a favor to follow some guy, okay? Like I owe her something."

"Don't you?"

"Nope. Never did. If I had, we'd be even now. More than."

And Mitch tells her a story.

"Where did they take her?" Dani says. "Why arrest her?"

"Don't *know* where they took her, Dani. And, I don't know. Fucking trespassing?"

"We have to get her out, then."

Mitch shakes her head. "I called. They said she's not at the jail."

Katherine's head lolls a bit. She leaves it there. Tightens her fingers on her bundle and gets a series of fast but controlled spasms in response.

"So," Dani says. "you know the man's address, then?"

Mitch goes to the kitchen and scribbles something onto some paper. Clips it onto the refrigerator with a look on his face like this is very funny. Dani nods and says she has to take a shower, leaves the room.

Katherine stands. Pushes herself as tall as she can to a series of cracks deep in her chest. The cracking feels wonderful.

Mitch spoons coffee grounds, pours water. He looks over to her occasionally, without moving the rest of his head. He thinks she doesn't notice.

The bundle containing her creature rests on the chair. It hasn't been moving much today, at least not since they got out of the car, where it stabbed her sides the whole time the wheels were turning. She still feels nothing there but the echoes of those piercing touches, but it's not pain.

She knows she should feel more. The space between her and the world of immediate sensory blasts and skittering confusion and a deep pulsating hunger grows wider very fast indeed, but isn't replaced evenly by normal feeling. Leaving gaps.

She's trying to reacclimate to people, after all the running and biting and hiding, but she has to look away every so often to recharge and finds herself looking at the outlines of her teeth in the carapace of her offspring. She's stolen back part of the life her body had given it. Stopped it in whatever process its life is a part of. A permanent or temporary cessation, and it feels like a fortunate ledge that saved her from a terrible fall, a relief to have found but too narrow to stay on for long.

"So, you've had a bad week of it," Mitch says. Tenderly, but his voice wobbles. Fear.

Katherine nods and sees him try not to flinch. She gets her head upright again.

"I mean Dani has that story. I haven't seen you in a few weeks. How much of that story is true?"

Katherine opens her mouth and breathes. It makes Mitch uncomfortable but he doesn't say anything. She runs her dry tongue over her dry lips until there's enough moisture for traction.

"All of it." Sound like a rattling inside her body she's not sure she likes. "As much as she knows."

"Yeah?" Mitch leans forward against the kitchen island. "There's more, then? What doesn't she know?"

Katherine isn't sure. "There was somewhere else. I went somewhere. Became something. Maybe it started before that."

Two limbs feel their way out of their sweatshirt wrapping. They wiggle in the air like antennae. The body itself doesn't move.

"The plasma center."

Katherine doesn't remember Dani saying anything about that. "Yes."

Mitch looks at the wall, the same direction as the creature but above it, like he's trying to see it without looking at it.

Katherine tenses, doesn't know why. It's an unfamiliar parental reflex, vague muscular warnings.

Mitch skirts the table, approaches the creature. Checks with Katherine.

She nods. She doesn't think he's in any danger.

Mitch walks closer than she expects, but still far enough to evince some caution. Crouches down and tilts his head, like if he can squint just right he'll get to the bottom of this.

The two waving limbs freeze in the air, stiff like dead tree branches, but Katherine feels the living tension radiating off them, thinks that Mitch can too.

The creature is marvelous and frightening, and Mitch's face goes back and forth between the options.

He starts to back up but the limbs do what they do, and quickly. Points dip into Mitch's skin and stay there. Brief tableau of every muscle in Mitch's body tensing at once, which is no way to move away from anything. Mitch jerks back but the ends of the arms hold him in place, like their narrow tips have somehow hooked into a load-bearing tendon.

Katherine swells with sticky human pride.

Mitch gets one quaver into a scream before the creature yanks its limbs from his body hard enough to tip itself off the chair and out of the sweatshirt, dead limbs dragging on the way down.

Katherine watches her offspring skitter in a confused and agitated circle, spending more energy than it has all day, and understands.

It got hold of the wrong flesh.

The creature's writhing grows more pained, starts to take up chunks of the carpet. Katherine goes to it. Is drawn to it. It reaches for her, more desperate than hungry. They have been striking a balance with each other, learning coexistence, since she arrested the process that would have ended her while completing it, setting up on this little in-between perch.

But the pull of those limbs, the frustrated moaning that she hears expressed in their scratching, it's not rage or violence but rather the barrier between what needs to be conveyed and what's communicable.

She moves toward the creature. Holds her hand out. The ends of the limbs still wet with Mitch's blood drag gently over her skin, raising goosebumps. Giving her the chance to pull away that they didn't give Mitch.

She doesn't take it.

The legs make their punctures and a rush fills Katherine's heads with thoughts, so many overlapping thoughts, and she reels, she blanks. Her mind washes white a moment under a flood of thought, of foreign minds.

It's only a moment, though, and then she comes back to herself, solid inside of the flood.

Then she starts to discern individual signals in the wave, the distinct variations of vibration that distinguish each voice from each other, and listens.

Somewhere, faint but there, is a very familiar voice.

Katherine can't identify the voice, but she starts to shake.

Dᴀɴɪ ᴛᴏᴡᴇʟs off and shrugs back into the same clothes she's been wearing for days. The steam creeps out the door and takes with it the brief sanity of Mitch's incongruously well-appointed shower, the water beaded on the glass door, blocking Dani's view of the chaos beyond. It was like muscles beneath her muscles unclenching for the first time.

But the air clears and her clothes scratch stiffly, suck the new clean off her skin, drag her back into the nightmare.

Back to Mitch sitting in the corner of kitchen, hugging his knees. In the living room, Katherine laying on her side on the floor, dead graying legs of the ribcage creature curling and flaking into their own hollows while the healthy black ones reach toward her.

Two of them wriggle under her. Glint of blood, and no, they wriggle *inside* of her. Blood beading down the carapace, sliding down toward the carpet and catching between the wick effect of the threads and the momentum tying it to the creature, hanging between the two and collecting until the building mass forces large drops onto the floor.

Dani's stomach twists and she lurches forward. Reaches for the creature against the strong advice of her stomach.

"Don't," Mitch says. "It's...something's happening. Like a bond, or something."

Dani wheels on him. "Are you—" but his face isn't high, isn't lazing sardonically at her. It's pale and gaping.

Dani steps well wide of Katherine and her pet, stops short of Mitch. Unclips the page of note paper from the fridge. Makes sure that she can read the handwritten address. It's clear on the other side of town, the university and downtown between.

Mitch stares at Katherine, mouth moving. But Katherine's mouth seems to be moving, too.

Or else the writhing from the intruding legs has gotten more intense, is vibrating through her body, moving the soft tissue of her lips.

Mitch is right. Something is happening. Katherine cranes her head like she's listening to distant voices.

Mitch wrote down the address like she asked, but now she doesn't know what to do with it. As though this Butler would go back, as though she'd find answers sneaking through his underwear drawer.

As if there wouldn't be more of those cops on site, if he did.

She crumples the note and stops short of the trash, tucks it into a kitchen drawer instead.

Katherine whispers, "Cora."

Dani freezes. Forces herself to unfreeze. Sits on the floor where she is and waits for whatever tragedy is coming.

Nothing much comes, though. More twitching from Katherine and Mitch sitting wide-eyed, about the way Dani is, probably. Then Katherine's eyes open and she scoops her creature up, covers it back up with the surf-themed hoodie from the gas station next to their motel room last night and holds it close.

Dani gives it a minute, two. Finally: "The cops don't have her."

Mitch blinks. "No. They say they don't."

"Who else in this town could?'

Mitch sighs heavy enough that it means he's already thought of this, already knows she's about to ask him to talk to whoever he still knows at the university.

MITCH HASN'T STOOD on this street in years, right outside the classroom building. Everyone's always just called it the classroom building, a three-story brick monster just north of the campus boundary, university property surrounded by the town like an enclave in a foreign country. It means he can just lurk across the street, though, and not be violating an order that may or may not still be in effect.

The Christian student center is in the same house it used to be, just across the street and down the block. His old union friend said to meet here. Mitch strolls in, trying to take five years or so off his walk, and pays the smiling clean-cut kid behind the counter for a paper cup. Same kind of friendly evangelical as always worked here, but they're nice and leave you alone and the push-top coffee dispenser surprisingly has about the best coffee in town.

Converting people with kindness, maybe, but Mitch is inclined to not be too cynical about it.

He goes out on the patio and takes a seat. Maybe a fresh coat of white paint on the porch since he's been here, a couple more rows of bike racks in the grass, but the same wrought-iron chairs and picnic tables, same porch a little too narrow for commercial seating to feel right.

He sips his coffee and slips back in time. Running into a professor on this patio, while he was mulling over grad school. The warning she'd given him, the deep aversion to caution he'd felt. How he realized he'd come to love being a student, finally, in the last year of college, staring through the steam of both cups and the smoke of his professor's guilty menthol.

He ignored the warning and enrolled for a few years, got involved in the union and met one of the few contacts he still has at the university.

She comes out of the classroom building surrounded by a little crowd, holding out a clipboard for signatures and passing out stacks of quarter-sheet flyers. Waves to the group to go on, she'll catch up with them, and marches to the patio, flops in the chair across from Mitch.

"I'll be damned, Mitch. You could have come to the meeting, you know."

"I just wanted to talk."

'Yeah, sure. I mean it can be tough coming back."

"Well..."

'You've got your exams set, then? I think that's where you were when it happened."

"I'm not exactly back."

The organizer looks around, at them, at where they are.

"I mean," Mitch says, "I'm not coming back. I just wanted to talk."

"What do we have to talk about?"

And Mitch gives it a go, says he remembers something about a unit on campus that wasn't covered by their contract even though they employed graduate students. He doesn't say that he thinks the university might be covering something with that blind spot, or that he's fixing to get himself on the wrong side of the university administration again.

The organizer's face tells him he doesn't have to.

"Damn it," she says. "It was bad enough when you got kicked out. The union took heat for that, you know?"

"Yeah, I never..."

"Campus cops knocking on our *doors*. A couple times, they didn't even knock."

He holds his hands out and says he thinks there's something going on that will affect all of them.

The organizer tells him exactly how much she thinks he cares about "all of them" and shoulders her bag and is gone.

Mitch settles back in his chair and takes a swig of his coffee, but he's missed the window on it and it's cooled to bitter. He could easily go in for a refill but plops the half-empty cup in the trash instead and heads out into the plaza, the upper guts of campus.

He's not supposed to be there anymore. Or he wasn't as of a few years ago. "Trespassed" was the word they used, repeating it like the strange usage made it more important, a binding magic spell. As in, "Do you understand you've been trespassed from campus?"

At the time, he had to consciously refrain from suggesting he might understand if they used words like normal fucking people. It wasn't a high point in his life, but even he could tell that wasn't going to help.

Now he's thinking he might have a chance to try that argument out.

The union organizer was the only live contact he could find in his phone. The others either had new numbers or wouldn't answer him.

Mitch wanders awhile, the layout of campus not coming back to him the way he expected. But he finds one bike trail that weaves around a couple trees, taking too wide an angle to be practical unless the landscapers expect the trees to quadruple in size, and he remembers a building a little way down that path, the handful of jobs that opened up one fall when construction was finished and his friend who said he'd rather do the front-desk thing than another round of introductory lectures on Weber and Polanyi. Maybe he's still there. It's a place to start, or at least something to do.

The bushes next to the building are all in bloom, perfectly crafted to give the look, combined with the mottled shade from the trees, of a cool spring day. But Mitch's shirt sticks to his back. He trudges along until a glass wall gleams through the greenery. He steps off the path and circles the building, trying to figure what door is the main entrance, the one where the reception desk would be.

He comes in and there's a desk all right, but the people behind it are impossibly young, chatting with each other in front of a sign for a department that doesn't even sound familiar, reads like academic mad-libs. He starts past them and finds the door locked.

"Appointment?" one of the clerks says.

Mitch tries out a name.

The other clerk types and scrolls. "Nobody by that name. Are you sure you're in the right place?"

"I mean, this used to have sociology offices."

The first clerk nods, tells him the name of another building. Much farther away. "This building hasn't had roaming offices in a few years, you know. Can I take your name?"

Mitch waves it off and gets back out the door. He's never heard of a campus building like that, with locks to keep you out of the hallways. It would be impossible to manage if there were classrooms in there, too many people for even a swipe-card system in that case, and this is all very sinister but he can't quite decide if it's important-sinister or just the way higher education has gone since his exit.

But then he gets around the first turn of the bike path, onto a little stretch between the backs of two buildings, fire escapes and air-conditioner units, and a man in a gray uniform appears in front of him. "I think you might be lost, sir."

"No, just got somewhere to be."

He tries to edge around the man, to not break his stride, but that's not the kind of conversation this is, and the man puts himself in front of Mitch and holds a hand out at chest level. Doesn't touch Mitch but gives him the opportunity to run into his hand.

Mitch declines.

"I don't believe you work here anymore, Mr. Annala."

Mitch raises his eyebrows, tries to act like he's affronted and not surprised by his name.

"If I'm not mistaken, you're trespassed from campus."

"That fucking word again."

This time the guard doesn't give him a choice, just puts his hands around Mitch's arm and marches him around back, toward a van Mitch had no chance to see.

Mitch looks for the cameras but he can't see them. They're there, though. Must be.

A ROOM like a hospital room but not a hospital room goes bright and then dim, starts to fade away. Not an even fade but fuzzing out from the center of objects, as though the clock and the chair and the surgical tray are windows. This is where Cora is, strapped to a table, but another scene pushes through, clawing in chunks to be seen, and she can't help but watch until it's resolved, developed edges and weight and it's not one scene, one place, but a series. A sequence she tries to keep up with. University Ave bars out on the west side of town. Rooftops and cars. Underside of a sewer grate. Living-room carpet drizzled with blood and ash, and hold there.

Something about that carpet, the smell coming off it. Or, not off it, but alongside it. Above it. There's a smell. Cora focuses on the smell, like focusing her eyes. It's the place where a living room meets a hallway.

Then the next place burns its way through that one. She tries to fight it, to focus on the carpet, but it's no use. A parking lot, stretching out like a desert before a row of chain stores. Then a cramped little garage full of children's bikes and power tools.

So many in-between places. Doorways to little rooms, things scuttling in the dark. She remembers the cold steel table and has no reason to believe she's not still there, except that she feels cool and dry. That doesn't fit the places she's seeing.

The hallway with the bloody carpet comes in again, the smell thick.

She's smelled that smell before, milder but detectable every place she's flashed to. Maybe she's been following it.

Unless, of course, she hasn't been following at all. The beginning of every fade feels like she's being pulled, like something's got its arm around her wrist.

The carpet gets sharper and Cora's stomach turns, wherever it is. The smell builds faster. In the other places, it was creeping in through the air, but here it's heavy and present, directional, and tied to a low persistent scratching sound. Cora tries to crane her head but that isn't how this works.

The direction she was aiming for creeps toward her in a long slow pan. Bloodstain swelling and spreading as the room does. A pair of feet and Cora gets a little dizzy, a disembodied head rush.

Black Doc Martens with the old-style rubber sole held on by the teamwork of staples and duct tape. Breaking leather on top where the toes bend.

Old blood caked along the leather. Cora does something like holding her breath. Watches as a widening field of vision reveals dirty socks, frayed jean cuffs, bloodied tee shirt. Katherine's face like a hole in the carpet and her tee shirt over a hole in her chest and a blackened ribcage pulsing in a sweatshirt pressed to her side.

Cora clenches and strains but the image is clear. Katherine breathes, and what's left of her chest stretches open.

And Katherine tilts her head up and locks eyes with Cora.

Cora's seen people in a few of her flashes so far, but none had noticed, looking around or through her. Katherine's eyes go wide, though, and her lips start moving.

Some kind of pointed-armed creature jabs another point shallow into Katherine's arm and Cora reels under a flood of images, a bloody storage locker and the shoulder of a nighttime highway and the backseat of a car and she starts to piece them together but feels Katherine slipping away before the image begins to fade.

SIX

Dani looks around Mitch's room, surprised. He's not the slob she would have expected. He doesn't seem to own anything. Maybe that's the key to neatness. Katherine, curled up in a small wooden chair, strokes the edge of the sweatshirt, staring at the creature. The green gore has solidified a bit, but not hard. Sickly gelatinous coat settling into the fabric.

She keeps stroking the sweatshirt. Like she thinks the sweatshirt is part of the body, or she's running through the motions of petting a cat but can't quite bring herself to touch the thing's shell.

"What do you remember?"

"Mitch asked me the same thing."

"Yeah?"

Katherine nods.

"What did you tell him?"

"I told him what I remembered."

Dani nods, realizes that that's not going to be quite enough. "And what was that?"

"What I remembered at the time. What...came to me."

"Can you tell me?"

"I don't remember them now. Not the same things."

Memories are stories, and stories require distance for the telling, and Katherine has none of that. It's like she's remembering physically. It makes her impossible to empathize with and perhaps impervious to interrogation.

Katherine frowns. "You wanted another answer."

"Yes, I think I did."

"I don't know what it is."

The creature senses something. Shifts in the sweatshirt, peels its way out the neck hole into the mustily conditioned air. Reveals the light poking through Katherine's chest to leave splotches on her tee shirt, like a peeling medieval painted halo dropped down to the gut.

"I saw Cora."

"You remember that?"

"Yes. It only happened yesterday."

"You *saw* her?"

"Yes. She wasn't there, but I saw her. Maybe where she is."

"What?"

"I don't know. I don't know how to tell you."

Dani points to the creature, only now realizing she has no way, really, to refer to the thing. "This...you started remembering things better after you..."

Katherine waits.

"You got some of your memories back a little once it started...*talking* to you, I guess?"

"Oh. Yes, right."

"Show me." Dani hooks her hands around the hem of her shirt, pulls it ungracefully over her head, murmuring muffledly through the cotton still over her mouth, "Show me how you saw her." Dani knee-walks her way over to

Katherine's feet. Leans into Katherine's knees, rests her forearms on her thighs.

Katherine slides her hand over top of her creature's torso. To protect Dani, maybe, or to protect the creature from her.

The creature doesn't hesitate. It scuttles across Katherine and down her legs, reaching two pointy arms out to prod at Dani's arms. She flinches but otherwise keeps still. The arms dip into her skin, withdraw, dip again. Her blood beads on her skin but it doesn't hurt. She waits for the pain to rush in after, after a delay the way it will if you cut yourself with a sharp enough knife, but nothing happens.

Dani licks her lips, dry-swallows. Thinks about mosquitos, of all things, the way their saliva keeps bites from itching until the bug's long gone. It's inexplicably soothing.

The needle limbs try again. Back legs shuffle.

Something isn't working.

The spider stretches itself out, vaguely kitten-like, legs on each of the chair's arms. Katherine closes her eyes. The back limbs catch on Katherine's sides and dig in.

Two needle arms raise like cobra's fangs over Dani's left arm almost too briefly to see and stab downward and Dani's head floats off in a blast of static.

The roar disperses to a solid white room. Gleaming walls, egg-crate ceiling. Dani wants to blink but it isn't that kind of vision. The white room burns her eyes awhile and a rush of other scenes cut into it, little gashes in the reality she's seeing:

A corrugated steel ceiling over beige plastic walls. Gone-brown blood smears running up toward the steel. The place she pulled Katherine from but after some drying and someone's stuffed a couple towels against the bottom of the door and peeled the hair from the dead woman's face.

Then: the uncovered ceiling bulbs and non-color carpet of the apartment Dani shared with Katherine sophomore year. It smells like garlic and olive oil instead of Katherine's sandalwood candles. Someone's skate shoes shuffle-step to music Dani can't hear at the edge of her vision, where the stove must still be.

Then: a dusty room, sickly near-dawn light. Tables and a duct-tape square marking off a stage for occasional local music, and the back room of Jim Jerry's looks far worse in the off hours.

But these rends through the world into familiar places fuzz out and dissipate, leave Dani looking into the same white room she started in and never quite left. All the smells of the other places she saw into linger a second, burnt garlic and copper blood and stale beer, until they're washed away by the cold medical smell of disinfectant and alcohol and smooth surfaces all around.

No sounds, here, except for an air-conditioner hum and a slow, occasional rustle of fabric. A slight shuffling sound she can't quite get a bead on. The light pushes harder into her brain. No way out of the glare.

The shuffling carries something under it. A murmuring underneath, almost a shushing sound. It resolves itself into syllables. Still incomprehensible. The syllables get a little louder, all consonants, until suddenly Dani recognizes Cora's voice.

The real world slams back but Dani is blind a moment. Carpet under fingers, light blasting the retina without leaving an appreciable image. Her body struggles to remember its functions and its borders. The carpet feels a part of her fingers until it begins to differentiate itself, peeling away without moving, and the sensation is almost painful.

Katherine dips her head down, stares into her eyes a long minute.

"Oh my god." Dani wheezes, whispers. "That's what it's been like? What you've been seeing?"

"Not seeing. It's..."

"I know."

"I see, still. At the same time. Like a...I don't have the words."

Dani remembers a room fading in, overriding images of other places, surging to make itself known. She gets it, doesn't have the words either.

But there's a lingering itch, a feeling of the world beyond this moment.

They sit there on the floor of Mitch's bedroom as the night starts to give way. Katherine's discomfort with speech is finally welcome, even comforting. Dani doesn't know what she would say, doesn't want to try talk about the tingling in the back of her skull.

The sky begins to lighten outside.

"I think I heard Cora," Dani whispers, not sure if Katherine's even awake.

Katherine lurches forward, elbows on knees. "Where?"

"I don't know."

"Oh. Yes."

WHILE DANI SLEEPS, long still intervals punctuated by groggy reaching for Katherine's hand, Katherine is swept in the wake of Dani's vision into a kind of mental twilight. This is like her own visions, a bit. She's seeing things that are or were real, or feel that way, but they're less clear than they were before. She can't make out the specifics of some of them, just a strong smell or a single visual detail. And with them she can feel what Dani feels. The creature has linked them somehow. A second set of feelings layered under her own.

Dani is terrified at her vision and, Katherine feels when Dani blinks awake briefly, mourning how Katherine has had to experience them on her own. It's such a welcome emotion that she can't quite parse, because she can't exactly remember what it was like to remember another way, to recall only what she experienced without this smattering of dispersed detail.

And her chest jolts like her heart's doubled its rate and her vision blurs out for a second in the manner of mild but bloody flesh wounds or standing up too fast. The floor jumps up to strike her cheek, dull pain only spreading out from the point of contact seconds later, and dimly.

She doesn't move for those seconds. Can't. Her creature scratches at the floor unhappily, circles and settles, waiting.

She's pressed to the floor by a physical sensation that shouldn't be physical, shouldn't trigger that set of nerves.

She knows which ones it should trigger, though, has gained enough awareness of her unfamiliar body for that.

It's grief and rage and panic sluicing down from the sky, to pin her to the floor. Coming from outside her body, making her toes tingle.

Dani reaches over half-awake, grabs a fistful of Katherine's shirt.

The rush of flattening emotion levels out a little and differentiates itself into its distinct feelings—claustrophobia, nausea, numb fingertips. Settles from the air outside her body into the parts of her body, furious pump of blood and the electric short-circuiting of the brain and rising panic adrenaline.

No breath is coming though Katherine gasps for it.

She can't move her arms or legs or head and her own eyes start to fade into another point of view, a new angle on the white-wall corner replacing her own. Mitch's bedroom becomes a peripheral ghost.

Men in some combination of medical and riot gear mill around, pressing at her sides and looking at her from the doorway. At least one pair of hands hold her shoulders down. Nervous hum in the room like the world's loudest power line.

Something clicks in the head she's in. The adrenaline drains, the light with it. Everything slows down. She tries to turn her head around, see who did what to make this happen, but she can't move at all and anyway all the masked and armored and gloved men are standing back, holding their hands up, looking at each other.

This drift into blackness is an inside job, coming from the body she's inhabiting, not its jailers.

With the dimming comes a sudden familiarity. By feel or by chemical proximity, she knows this is Cora. This is what has happened to Cora.

These men have seen her coming to life and tried to dim her back to sleep.

But something comes crashing from Cora. Katherine's face breaks out in sweat. Her throat seizes and Cora is not going to sleep and a static speaker crackles and then a honking alarm and then Katherine is back in Mitch's bedroom.

Dani whispering loudly, pointlessly. Katherine moves her jaw side to side. Dani shakes her and the creature stands suddenly tall, raises its front legs in a threat. Dani holds her hands up, pushes away from Katherine.

The front legs go down but the creature doesn't settle all the way.

"Something is happening," Katherine says when she can manage it.

"Are you okay?"

"Cora."

"Cora?"

"Something bad. Violence, needles…I don't know. She felt so strong. I think I know where she is."

DANI DRIVES. Katherine talks to her at first, guiding her along, but after a few turns Dani starts to see what Katherine is seeing and doesn't need the copiloting anymore. It's a burning signal in her internalized sense of the city. She can't tell exactly what's around it, what building they're going to. She doesn't know the southeast end of campus that well. But that's where the signal's coming from and so she cuts down 34th and then the campus road past the museum.

Early morning haze and empty sidewalks. The sun hasn't yet made good on its threat but is advertising its arrival. They only pass early-bird go-getters and up-all-night paper writers, maybe one a block. There will be more students soon, but for now it's the tail end of a quiet campus weeknight.

The signal tugs on Dani so she turns left into a maze of little one-way streets with parking spaces cut into the side.

Five spaces and then a planter with a palm tree. She keeps as straight a heading as she can, past the classrooms and offices, until they're close enough that she can locate the signal inside a structure.

Katherine stiffens, feels it too.

Dani drives under a glass skybridge between two buildings. On the left, an old one, the kind of heavy university-gothic architecture she's always loved in spite of herself. Brick aging into a uniform color, concrete slabs poured on either side of stairwells. On the right, a modern riff on the form, a tall stack of bricks with one corner in glass as though a giant took a hot knife to the building, carved an even hunk of brick away and carefully patched it with glass.

The newer building looks like millions of new dollars, flashy in a plausible-deniability sort of way, and sits atop a burning in Dani's mind.

Around back of the building there's a little loading dock and a couple parking spaces. Some kind of sign telling them who can park there. Dani ignores it and parks and they pile out of the car. Dani starts shaking. Latent rush of her body answering her new sight or something she's picking up from Katherine, or just plain adrenaline, but she waits a second. Steadies enough for Katherine to lean against her enough to even out her own peculiar gait.

They shuffle inside, through heavy wood doors onto new tile floors set in a big old-fashioned diamond pattern. The air conditioning is sharp and cold and vibrates on Dani's skin. Cora's signal, physical this close. They circle around to the front of the building, the main entrance, and there's no reception desk. It's not that kind of building. It's got department offices on this floor, classrooms up above.

Dani's surprised. She was sure that this far south on

campus, this close to several branches of the campus hospital, this would be a medical facility.

They circle the floor until they come to an open double door with a curved desk just inside. Dani starts to shuffle past but Katherine freezes in the doorway, staring. Dani curses and pulls them both inside.

It's faculty offices. The sign says Chemistry Department, Standish Hall. There's a young man in a school-colors purple polo behind the counter, definitely supposed to greet them and help them find whoever they're here to look for, give them information on majoring and maybe some handouts about course offerings and the student club, but he's got his head down on the desk, blood pooled in front of him.

Dani wheels around but there's no one in the hallway, no one approaching. The student must have been the first in this morning, probably just opened the office when Cora's signal got to him.

Katherine pushes off Dani's shoulder and tiptoes toward the kid. Dani tries to call her back without speaking. It must get through because Katherine looks back and shakes her head. Puts her hand on the kid's shoulder. He stirs, reaches up a finger and twists it in his ear. Squeaks some blood out and looks at it clumped on his finger and slumps back down.

Katherine steps back, eyes wide. This is Cora's cry for help, ripping through everyone in the building. Soon that will be more people by far, students and professors filing in for the first class of the day, and who's to say that Cora's done screaming.

A rumble comes through the floor, a bright pulse in the back of Dani's eyes.

There's a basement.

They come out into the hall again, head for a stairway

by the far door. Dani walks slow and waits for something to happen.

The stair door swings open.

Squelch of shoes and a slow patter. Dani and Katherine freeze where they are. A man in body armor with an empty holster on his belt hauls himself through the doorway, bent low like he's climbed for miles. A set of gashes through his neck leave thick strips of flesh swaying with his movement. Little strands of kelp waving in blackened gum where blood ought to be gushing.

Dani doesn't breathe and Katherine doesn't either. A deep cold radiates off the man, the body, familiar but completely foreign. Whatever almost happened to Katherine, whatever changes she's shared with Dani, have their extreme counterpart in this walking corpse, this shredded neck and putrefying flesh still upright.

He doesn't see them, but another set of hands grip the doorway behind him, then another. A person with a caved-in mouth, gummed over in red mesh like his damaged flesh started to re-stitch itself, and a stomach torn wide where one of the kidneys would be. Another with eyes pushed in, leaking purple gunk down his cheeks and settling in globules under his jaw like foul earrings.

The dead shamble in place, squishing blood in their shoes but not looking over at Dani and Katherine. Dani flinches back. If this is what Cora's panic has done here, maybe they should leave, let it sort itself out.

Katherine snaps at this mentally, a push of pure objection. And Dani agrees. But it's hard to hold her ground.

And though they can both sense that what happened to these men is kin to what's happening to them, there's no shared feeling, no connection like the one they have with each other. They are a void.

Another set of hands on the doorframe, stiff fingers straining until finally a body crests the threshold, feet kicking feebly behind. This person sprawls in a hospital gown and a confusion of limbs and hair, slides to a stop against the wall.

The three mutilated bodies snap their heads up toward Dani and Katherine, jumping to attention and coming into a formation around the newcomer.

Katherine recognizes her before Dani does.

Two of the bodies pull Cora to her feet. She struggles her head up groggily. Pupils swallowing irises.

Katherine holds up a hand, hailing, inviting recognition.

Cora cocks her head like a marionette. Like Katherine when Dani first found her, but more physically intact. No gaping wounds, anyway. Blank eyes, someone else's blood pattering off her fingertips.

"Cora," Dani says.

Cora twists her face around to square with Dani's voice. The three corpses shuffle around until they're facing Dani. Cora looks curious, maybe, or just wounded, and Dani belatedly notices the IV needles half-torn from her arms, the raw red bands around her wrists.

Katherine steps forward and the three tense and silently snarl.

Katherine retreats and they settle.

They're a barrier.

Cora's killed some of her captors and made them her bodyguards.

The air conditioner kicks over and hums.

The door at the end of the hall crashes open and thuds hard against the wall. Gets held open for several men to flood through. Living men, armed and armored. Boots thunk their way in. Three in view before anyone reacts.

Tactical helmets and big two-hander guns. Dani ducks toward the wall and Cora's corpses shuffle around, reverse their semicircle to face this new threat, but Katherine just swallows and rubs her hand on her creature's carapace.

The first living man holds up one commanding hand. The others stop but the hand shakes. They touch their holsters, wait. The lead man pops the button on his and lowers himself a little.

Katherine sways, rocks back and forward and lets her creature go. It shoots off her hands as though she had thrown it, finally touching the ground only to slide, give a quick skitter. Projects itself forward. The corpses don't seem to even register it skirting their feet, making a wavering beeline. Compensating for the way its damaged legs make it curve gradually off track by pulling a quick twirl every several steps, correcting against the curve with a tight curlicue back the other direction.

The living men pull their guns too slow. This is not a threat they were ready for. A bullet splinters the floor. Another punches a hole in the marble wall.

Dani's ears ring from gunfire and university-gothic acoustics. A riot cop finally pulls of another shot and blows off a chunk of the corpse to the Cora's left. It rocks side to side but doesn't flinch or fall. Katherine's creature darts between that cop's legs and spins a quick circle behind him and plunges its two front legs into his calves.

The man screeches and falls. His scream changes pitch before he hits the ground, becomes more the tension between muscles and passing air than an expression of pain. The ground meets him hard and he doesn't move.

The cops turn toward each other and stop just shy of putting holes in their allies. Scan the floor where the creature just was. Nothing doing. They pull their rifles up toward Katherine and the creature pulls itself out from under the fallen man's chest and swipes its front legs at their ankles.

It catches one of each of them. Punctures the skin and hooks on Achilles tendons. Then it's a matter of leverage, bracing all the other pincer legs against tile enough to pull and saw and rip. A gun goes off, into the ground. The walking corpses dive onto Cora as a shield. The creature finishes ruining ankles and the two guards tip into each other, onto the floor.

Cora's crew surges forward to finish the job, drive their gooey fingers into the guard's throats, leaving flecks of their own failing flesh on the guards' skin until fresh blood rushes from their throats. Rise from their work and kind of lean toward Cora. Plants following sunlight. Dani's legs burn and she stands from the crouch she's been holding, staring half-deaf at the pooling blood.

Cora lurches toward Katherine, flanked by her guards. Katherine steps towards her, feeling something like reunion, like the touch of familiar skin, even if she can't quite put words to the feeling, but the corpses spring to their feet and form a wall.

"We have a car," Dani says, unsure if anyone else in the hallway can even process words right now. "I think we can fit everybody in but we need to go right fucking now." She listens for sirens and doesn't hear any. It's worse, somehow. There won't be any sirens, she doesn't think. Just more men, an endless stream of men, pouring through doorways pointing guns.

Maybe Cora reacts and maybe she doesn't, Dani is done guessing. She turns on her heel with a mental shout to Katherine and footsteps follow them out.

She opens the passenger door for Katherine and eases

her into the seat. Cora's in no shape for tests of her coordination but her three new friends have tagged along as well. They wait in something like a pile for Dani to open the back door, leaning on and supporting each other's weight and then trying to get through the door all at once to fill the seats intended for, at best, two and a half people.

Dani steps back and watches them sort it out in a mass of loosening flesh and unnaturally solid blood. They clump together somehow in the backseat, the boundaries between their bodies seeming to dissolve. Squishing against each other harder than should be possible, forming one solid mass with Cora unaltered in the middle.

They condense enough that the door closes easily for Dani. She gets in the front seat. Drives. Watches for cops and doesn't take another breath until they cross the road at the east end of campus and drain out into the arteries of Palm Gulf.

Dani bursts from the car and sucks in heavy mouthfuls of damp air. The Florida humidity for once comes as a pleasant change, the way it clings to the mouth and throat replacing by gradual degrees the death-smell of the enclosed car she's been driving around town for the last half hour, reluctant to stop but moving without a destination.

She knows the heavy air is the product of a different decay than what's in the car, has said at any number of parties and first dates that this state and its major attractions, its year-round balminess and aggressive greens, were nothing more than the visible signs of rot, of death that never freezes. St. Augustine grass papering over liquified flesh, palm trees sucking dilute blood up from the dirt to fan over highways and front lawns.

She has to admit now that there's a difference, though. The life cycle, the subtropic fecundity, smothers the peninsula under its weight until even the wildlife is compressed into narrow-tailed squirrels and scrawny racoons, but the accelerated above-ground version filling the car is a different story. It scores grooves into her nostrils and she can still smell it, no matter how far she walks across the parking lot.

It's fitting, maybe, that they've wound up in the Speak-Script lot, the same strip mall as the plasma center. There's a bitter joke, as old as the one about returning to the word mines when the cigarette was spent, about how no one escaped the place. People left for new jobs, hot opportunities, but sooner or later wound up struggling with the same dying-before-their-time keyboards, astonished at how quickly they remembered the *annuity* and *whole-life insurance* hotkeys.

They'd take you back, if you hadn't burned the bridge too badly, after the internet company went under or the exam-prep job was a bust, and they never called references. You'd take up smoking again and start stretching out your shifts, remember your preferences for workstations.

But Dani remembers one week, when a punk festival drew people from across the country into town in minivans and airport shuttles, claiming they'd spent the week hitch-hiking and hopping freight trains. There was a van parked in this lot. It was painted in the old hippie designs, unfashionable enough that they were certainly handmade knock-offs and not store-bought nostalgia. It stayed in the lot for the whole week.

Generally speaking, body odor is not heavier than air,

does not linger in an open strip-mall lot for days at a time. It told her then that neither the cops nor anyone else was enforcing the authorized-parking-only sign at the edge of the lot.

So this is where she's stopped, parking between Speak-Script and the art supply store, and stumbled to the edge of the lot and didn't vomit, not quite.

She's gasping, though, and good as the air feels she's getting a late-night-whiskey feeling in her gut. Mouth watering, eyes burning. She braces herself against a parking sign and tries to calm her diaphragm.

She spits and lights a cigarette. The last few weeks have helped her cut down at last. The smoke tastes more like ash than she remembers. Every capillary and vein in her body constricts, or feels like it, and her head swims a little.

Moderation has its moments.

She gets her stomach under control and sucks down the rest of her smoke. Feels Katherine getting a little dizzy from the shared nicotine experience back in the car. She never was a smoker. Dani grinds the butt out on the loose pavement and knows she has to go back to the car. Hopes everyone's stayed inside, hasn't piled out in their varying states of intactness.

Instead of a cloud of corpses standing around the lot when she comes back around the corner of the strip mall, however, she only sees the car. Several silhouettes sitting quietly, heads forward. Waiting, if they've even noticed her absence and thought it strange.

The driver-side door lets out the stench she was trying to escape. Maybe a little worse, with the building heat. Dani rides her nicotine high through her gag reflex.

No one's moving, no one's talking. Five sets of eyes point straight out the windows, but she feels Katherine's nervousness like a physical itch. The sentient corpses on either side of Cora in the backseat lean a little bit forward, like someone reached back to touch Cora and they got defensive, want to make sure that such an intrusion doesn't happen again.

"Where do we go?" Dani asks, largely to herself.

Katherine doesn't answer or shrug or point. Scans her eyes around the strip mall. Dani follows suit. Plasma clinic and SpeakScript and art supply store and vacant slot. Beige stucco walls and windows on their third set of branded stickers, the archeology of failed businesses.

As it ever was.

Dani remembers something and turns her head. Stops midway to let the corpses unclench their muscles, decide once again she's not a threat. Twists the rest of the way to look at the pawn shop that's still back there across Sixth Street, neon-paint paisley and mushrooms and bars across the windows.

And an *open* sign notably not lit.

She can't remember it ever being lit. Used to be, she'd joke at the other smokers and break-takers at SpeakScript about how it was surely a mob front, a money-laundering gimmick.

But something about it looks different now. It's more empty than it used to be.

"Hey," Dani says, "we need a place to hide out, right?"

Katherine remembers enough of what used to be regular life to be surprised by the dust. It's heavy. Not long-time-derelict heavy, but certainly a couple weeks of heavy, and she tries to think of a way to tell this to Dani.

It's not that easy, though, and she can't feel Dani's thoughts quite as clearly as Dani seems to be cued into hers. Dani's running her hand over the display cases, though, lifting things up to look at them like a performance just for herself.

They must have roughly the same idea.

And it gives her something to think about besides Cora.

All Cora's footsteps echo behind her, her original feet and her six auxiliary ones, progressing in sloppy lockstep through the display room. Dani's wondering about the door locks and whether passersby could see them from the back alley, but Katherine is pretty sure the decision has already been made in the stark track Dani's finger made on the glass, the way she looked down at it like she didn't quite believe. The still air, the window tint that isn't noticeable from the street.

Does it matter if you remember who you are, if you know in which direction you are heading? Is it important to check yourself against all the baggage of your past, to make sure you really mean what you're doing, if all that's been left to you is right now, a leaky torso in a dusty room and a vague sense against all odds that there might be more of you?

It is, for Dani. It does. She keeps looking, and Katherine has no intention of stopping her.

She's already settling in herself, though. Thinking about which corner of the shop will be hers.

Maybe not here in the front room, what used to be the display room. Maybe a front in more ways than one, as Dani likes to suggest, though Katherine is coming around to other ideas about decay and abandonment, dust and why it settles, that are at once more and less sinister than what's arresting Dani.

No one is coming back here. It's an abandoned building. It has that smell.

The front room is partitioned by the display case, an office behind the back wall. If you were standing behind the glass case or the cash register, separated from the wider browsing lanes with their low shelves and telegraphed security cameras, there'd be another barrier you could slink behind, through a little push door that's standing open now at the outer end of its swing.

Katherine leans her way around the corner and braces against the doorjamb, hears her creature skuttling along on the other side of the counter, out of sight but keeping close. The effort of holding herself up has started to wear on her. A soreness in her torso, on top of the dull ache of her spine, the places her ribcage has been severed. The back and oblique muscles overcompensating to keep her even mostly upright.

There's another tiredness, one she hasn't even begun to settle up with. She's been touching the edges of the wound lately, on the car ride over, but can't even think about it now without her knees going weak.

She settles in the corner of the office, cocks one knee up for her creature to circle around and lay down under. Rubs the dust away with her elbows, the seat of her pants. Feels herself changing the structure of the place with that contact. A growing clean spot the more she touches, dirt clinging to the fabric of her clothes.

It's an exchange, being in a new place. A navigation between surfaces, an exhalation of moisture and a disturbing of sediment.

Katherine tries to think about how she feels. This was

an important question for Dani, she remembers, when she first pulled her out of the storage unit. Like the answer would give Dani the way forward, a map to where Katherine was. What had happened to her and how bad. It doesn't mean much to Katherine. She can process sensations, of course, can pick up what her body's telling her moment-to-moment, but that's not what the question's after. It's after something deeper, something insulated from the circuit of output and input situated in a place, and she doesn't recognize that idea much anymore.

But as her set of inputs and outputs rapidly expands, so does what her body remembers as it collects something like a set of feelings.

Cora comes in the door, flanked and followed by her three new friends, and Katherine realizes it's the first time that there hasn't been another body between the two of them in a long time. She smiles, unworried about whether the gesture is tracking right. She just smiles.

Cora limps over, discolored skin and frozen face, but Katherine feels something coming off her, like an icy wind from way far below, but she thinks it's like her smile. The best Cora can do.

Cora walks up to just outside of arm's reach and crouches down, studies Katherine or looks like she does. Her guard stands behind her, rocking a little. Side to side, like they're waiting under duress, don't think anything good will come of this.

Katherine straightens up her head, nods to signal she knows the effort Cora's making and appreciates it.

Cora stares. Blackened eyes and peeling lips. Katherine watches and waits, but Cora doesn't move.

Katherine badly wants to reach over and peel the hair off her forehead, this person whose smell she still knows.

Cora's further gone than she ever was and far quicker. Expressionless, but that doesn't bother Katherine. She taps herself on the chest, nods twice. Holds her arms out to show there's no more damage than she came in with, anyway.

Katherine finds herself waiting for a clear recognition, a signal that the relief at finding each other is mutual.

Instead, Cora walks backwards into the corner. Her guard closes in around her and she's gone from view.

Out in the other room, Dani is running her fingers over the links in a gold bracelet, the charms alternating between initials and dolphins, imagining the life that kicked it out to keep itself going. Katherine wants to go and help her, but whatever's coming off her isn't the kind of thing that needs talking about.

Katherine's content to sit here in the back room of the pawn shop, waiting with the rest of the flotsam.

SEVEN

THE FACTS ON THE GROUND, AS BUTLER UNDERSTANDS them:

The Institute got its start in fields far from secret civilian testing of ancient biological material, as a private financial interest seizing control of foundering university departments with very conditional donations.

The Institute started with economics departments. If you're funding the department, and have an operative writing from inside, you can get most anything published under university letterhead, whether the author has academic credentials or not. This lends credibility to the sorts of government policies that create more foundering university departments, which makes more room for the Institute to operate.

The next places cleared for takeover, and probably part of the goal all along, were earth sciences departments. The extraction of natural resources must proceed unabated, and the semiprivate university subdivisions help grease the wheels of commerce, and here the Institute had even less trouble. Joint funding and private-public partnerships

became Institute research units became Institute departments, with money fueling the process and consolidating as
a result of it. Control over faculty hiring and research
funding let the Institute decide very quietly on what
climate science did or not consist of.

Which led to the specimen.

White describes the extraction of methane from frozen
underground deposits in calm clear language that makes the
process perfectly understandable when he's speaking but
allows the details to kind of fade from the memory when
he's done.

The specimen came out of one such frozen deposit,
mined by an Institute deep-sea installation. The mining
operation slowed to a crawl as the Institute developed a way
to carve it out without puncturing the organism or over-
heating the methane, ensure a research opportunity instead
of an oceanic fireball.

Eventually they managed it. Anyone else would have to
develop their own extraction process, but if there are more
of the specimens they will be found. The drive for control
of resource extraction eventually leads underwater.

So the release of the creature into the world became
inevitable as soon as it was discovered. Any company faced
with a discovery of this magnitude is under market pressure
to find a use for it before the competition does or be over-
taken. The race is on.

If there are bioweapon applications, the Institute needs
to be the first to develop them. If the symbiont leads to
medical advancements, the Institute needs those patents.
And if the exploitation of ocean resources unleashes a
plague of the creatures, perhaps more aggressive or larger
than the one they've found, the Institute will have a cache

of solutions ready, and the contacts and patents and facilities to control these applications.

So when White tells him that it's time for him to see the specimen, Butler remembers the other fact he's pretty sure he knows: the oily lump White showed him in an above-ground room of this building, how it spread thin over the bottom of its biohazard enclosure. How it looked inert at first, until White put his hands into the inbuilt gloves and moved them, and the specimen rapidly found itself a shape and seized on the moving hands. How quickly that reflex could carry the specimen across the world, cutting through societies and biomes until nothing outside its influence remained.

"I have seen it."

"You've seen a sample."

Butler's face goes numb.

White leads him through featureless corridors, down deeper underground than Butler thought the building would go, to a door that White swipe-cards and key-pads open on a room with a wall of glass ten feet in. Butler squints around, gathers that it's a massive glass chamber, reaching up and through the ceiling.

White holds his hand out, an arch suburban dad showing off his new car. Doesn't touch the glass, though, and nearly whispers.

"Do you see the difference, where the shadows are darker than they should be?"

Butler peers, nods.

"Put your finger to the glass."

Butler hesitates, then does it. The glass is freezing, but in the space between his brain screeching its impulse to pull back and his actually doing it the shadows rush forward. He rubs his hand on the leg of his slacks to warm his fingers and the darkness is already receding to its corner.

Butler is left with afterimages of impressions, a sense of gelatinous limbs and a massive body, crushing into more than squirming over itself. A vague green hue Butler knows well from his early patients, the blood that would ooze and spurt when the weight of the hosts broke the symbionts' limbs before they developed, and from the hotel room of his most recent failed patient.

"You can see why we draw from the smaller sample," White says.

"Have we...?"

"Introduced subjects to the entire specimen? Yes. Early trials. They were less useful, but conclusive. Very nearly complete losses. Some survived. We have them kept secure. Catatonic. They certainly still have some connection to the organism. Their bodies have changed, and they look dead but still respond to any stimulus related to the organism. You've seen minor versions of those changes in some of your subjects."

White leads him back up into the world. His car is waiting.

The Florida air is sweet, the traffic on the streets and sidewalks for once more than a crushing collection of bodies, a parade of genetic materials and bacterial micro-biomes and respiratory functions pushing along each other in mass right-of-way flows mirroring their component parts. Butler can buy in, for now, to the people all around him as discrete individuals, with their own paths and their own decisions to make.

The grooves will soon make themselves known again, though, the locked-in systems, as inside so outside, grinding each vessel down until it stops. Butler has familiarized himself with the grooves, couldn't forget about them if he wanted to. Sees them projected all around.

The plasma center, smack in the middle of all this teeming motion, could alone produce results where secret labs and sterilized equipment and controlled variables couldn't, could keep the subjects developing past the point of initial contact.

White hinted that production is the product of control.

Butler is coming to a very different conclusion.

The best lab in the world can't recreate what he has here, in a Sixth Street strip mall, in all its dirt and chaos and motion. People moving, grinding along against the edges of their grooves, testing at the boundaries but never really going anywhere new, that's where the creature can develop. It needs its hosts to be in motion, to be living as well as alive. That's what was needed to develop the symbiont, a position in the center of the whole teeming hive.

That's what created this new symbiont, what identified and put in play its host, and what will be needed to find them.

The downside has become apparent. The Katherine patient, and the little crew around her, her friend who came looking and who knows who else. Butler had been considering the worst possible outcome to be her death and discovery, the eventual asking of unwanted questions and need to put the research on hold.

But there's a new possibility. Katherine, out in her grooves again but with one major alteration. If she's not dead than she must have help; if she has help than the problem is only going to spread.

Butler stands out front of the plasma center, keys in his hands. The sun's up in a pale sky, dewy air and motor exhaust, and he takes a deep breath. Settles in. The first cars start turning into the lot, not *like* clockwork but *a kind of clockwork*, the first gears in the machine to turn.

The plasma center door opens easily, habitually, and Butler slides in, replaces the bolt behind him. Not control, then, not rigor, but pressure on the grooves. Ride the machine where it's going but introduce one new thing

Butler makes his way to the back room, carrying an armload of new equipment in latched dry boxes, courtesy of White and the Institute. He has much work to do, and only two hours before the patients and staff arrive. The Institute has given him new tools. He suspects that only he sees how to use them.

ARMED WITH A BRIEFCASE newly stocked with fresh needles and some new tools, and an ice-water-compressed face because the bruising is less noticeable than his attempts at concealing it, Butler sets out to contact the patients who've had the orange needles to determine whether any of them show signs of the symbiont changing their physiology. If they've started to change since their last visits, recent events might pull Butler's attention from checking up on them until it's too late, until the spread has worsened, and he can't afford that kind of surprise.

Still less can he afford the kind of surprise where someone else visits them first.

The first two houses, no one's home. Butler thinks about leaving a calling card and smiles to himself about it, knocks a third time instead. The second address is up in the fourth cinderblock floor of an apartment building. Butler only knocks the once, has the feeling that the hallway is watching him.

He'll have to circle back, maybe try to find out when the subjects are likely to be home.

The third subject opens his door, up-and-downs Butler like he can't believe what he's seeing. Butler is at least holding his little black doctor's bag, in the hope that appealing to some children's-book idea of how a doctor arrives would put the man at ease.

It doesn't. They both know where they know each other from.

The man lets him in eventually but looks all over the neighborhood while he does it, as if someone watching would know who Butler was and still be in a position to get supercilious. Keeps looking everywhere but Butler during the pitch, the supposed mistake with their blood-testing contractor requiring Butler to draw blood for an additional safety test.

Butler says he knows the man's clear but they have to maintain their license. Of course he'll be compensated for his time. If the man buys it, he doesn't show it, but he puts his arm on the kitchen table and bleeds into a tube for a few seconds, then reaches across for the fifty-dollar charge card Butler slides across the table.

It is, perhaps, the eternal gambit: pay someone for a part of themselves but always pretend you're only paying for their time.

Butler waves as he heads down the front steps, but the man stares out his screen door hatefully. Nothing to be done about it now, and certainly it would have been better to call ahead, but it has never before occurred to him that his subjects don't think of themselves as the kind of people who have to sell a part of their blood. The man didn't want that part of his life, the part he slips into when he can't make it through the days until the next paycheck, intruding into the rest of it, what he probably thinks of as the normal part. It's absurd. Butler has the man's records, and to be selected to be part of this study there has to be a clear regularity in visits, a certainty that the person will visit at least every couple of months for monitoring.

The man isn't even aware of his predictability, can't see the grooves of the track his life runs along. Must think every month is a new chance to avoid Butler's clinic, a fresh opportunity for things to be different.

Maybe this ought to make Butler feel for the fellow. It doesn't.

Butler drives around the block before parking and going to the trunk. This is all too slow, the odds he'll walk in on someone at the crucial moment too slim. The mistake would be losing focus on the grooves, trying to figure out each individual subject.

Butler is going to have to change his focus to speed things along.

He rummages into the back of the trunk and pulls several towels off his briefcase, the one with the new tools, lugs it back to the driver's seat. He opens it, untangles a thick mass of cords and cables. Uncovers a small circular computer mounted in foam and surrounded by electrodes and wiring. Butler leaves alone the components he doesn't know what they do. He only knows the device, a developmental tracker, from a brief demo White gave him on a prototype mounted into a console at the Institute. It wasn't like the GPS on a car, wasn't two points in space and a more or less direct line between them. More like meteorology, color-coded circles within circles, heavy-activity patterns the brightest red, then pink areas with lower but detectable activity, and gray where the device can't pick anything up.

Somehow it detects exposure to the symbiont like radar, color-codes the probability someone affected is in a given area.

White had said that the parameters for a person registering vary depending on a host of variables that the Institute is in the process of dialing in. Hence the prototype. It's possible that as little as brief physical contact with an infected person or even breathing the same as air one could register on the device, but that's still more specificity than his little patient list.

Butler switches the power source on, but bringing the thing to life will require a little of him, a link to his body as a receptor.

The interface is a heavy braided cable running from the computer, locked in place with a plastic zip tie. Hard plastic disc on the end of it with a sharp nub in the middle. Butler strokes the sides of the nub. He's careful not to touch the point but does anyway. Pricks the skin. Blood welling up from the pad of his thumb.

He curses. Sucks the bead of blood off his thumb. Hooks the nub through the skin on the back of his hand, holds it for a three-count, pulls it out again.

The screen hums to life, gray flooding to a uniform pink and then starting to differentiate. A rough map of the city, digital lines where major streets are, and some pink smearing around red hot spots.

Butler stares at the shapes clarifying, the number of red heavy-intensity zones. He knew his patients lived all over town, but the representation of the infected spaced out like this, sprawled across the city into neighborhoods a dozen miles or more from his clinic, the smearing trace of the contact they make, is something different.

He thinks about his grooves, the tracks his patients' lives move along.

He needs more specificity, which will require more power to the machine.

He wipes the blood off the prong out of a mechanical sense of cleanliness and takes a deep breath and holds it. Rolls his head to the side and waits until the world starts to swim before jabbing the nub into the flesh behind his earlobe. Twisting until it feels secure and exhaling as hard as he can to carry the sting out with the air.

After an initial flare, it hurts less than he thought it might, but the feeling of the plastic in his skin is unshakable. Won't fade or become familiar. Then the piercing feeling jumps directly into his brain and spreads across his scalp.

He grinds his teeth until the screen lights up brighter, a blast of red pixels, narrowing and sharpening, leaving pink echoes behind, finally forming the weather-pattern shapes he needs. The display is fine, but his vision itself is already changing, the information from the interface seeping underneath the world he sees with his eyes. Some fiddling with the control panels built into the sides of the computer get the shapes moving, and he points his car in the right direction.

White had warned him not to do this except in an emergency, and then to only leave the interface connected for long enough to point himself in the right direction. The situation is worse than that, though. He has a world to save. He leaves the prong in his neck.

BUTLER's new sight is wonderful. Clarifying. It gives structure to the surface of the city, shows how its parts have moved to come to where they are, which suggests where they might go next. A patient stopped at a coffee shop but only once and not recently, a dim rusty shade; a frequented bus stop glows more intensely.

The house Butler passes glows most brightly, red bleaching to white. He pulls around the block and starts to remove the plug from his head, but the neighbors here won't know him. If they do, he could pass it off. A fancy hearing aid, maybe, or an anti-nausea device.

And he likes the augmented sight too much to surrender it.

So he hefts the suitcase in his hand, tucks his prop doctor's bag under the same arm, and closes the car door. The street is quiet and shady, trees arcing above cracked foundations and off-kilter front stairs. The street would be historical if anything had been preserved, but all the important houses are miles north, on larger lots, and these old buildings swell with moistened wood and give up their paint in flakes.

Before he rounds the corner, though, the shabbily picturesque street quavers. Shimmers like a hot highway and threatens to blur all the way out. A sharp click in the back of his skull snaps his vision sharp again. The house has a hard edge now, an outline setting it apart from the rest of the street.

Butler walks the half a block to the house. Knocks on

the door three times. Someone shuffles inside. He knocks again.

"Not right now," from inside, muffled.

Butler knocks again.

"Just leave the damn flyer or whatever. Swear to god I'll read it."

Butler tries the knob. Unlocked. He steps into a dim entryway and closes the door behind him before the man on the couch pulls his face out of the throw pillow.

"Hey, what the fuck?" The man rolls over on his back, holding his stomach.

"Jack Freemont?"

The man snorts. "Get the fuck out of my house."

But it's him. The new eyes in Butler's eyes see a red halo around him.

"Mr. Freemont, I'm sorry to intrude."

The man clenches his gut like he's trying to get up, but all he winds up doing is make his face go slack. He rolls over to face the back of the couch, groaning.

It gives Butler plenty of cover to slip his hand inside his doctor's bag for the syringe and take a few steps closer.

"Mr. Freemont, I promise I'm here to help. I understand you're in some pain. Can you describe your symptoms to me?"

"You're not my doctor."

"You don't have a doctor."

Mr. Freemont pauses his groaning long enough to hear Butler's last few steps. He catches sight of the appliance on Butler's neck and starts to push himself away, but it's too late. Butler hooks his elbow around the man's neck and pins one arm with his knee and comes down with the syringe. Has to try a couple times to get the vein. Blood in narrow rivers down Mr. Freemont's arm.

Buter pulls a sample and removes the needle, doesn't bother to put pressure on the wound. "Mr. Freemont, this will help us determine what's happening to you."

Mr. Freemont look down to his wound, holds it up to Butler like an accusation, and then doubles up so hard he pitches off the couch, leaves a smear of blood down the cushions.

"I am sorry about this," Butler says, putting the vial in his bag. "If it had happened according to schedule, we would have been better able to take care of you."

"You *did* this to me."

Butler nods mechanically. "I am sorry."

He pulls his phone out and dials White's office, notifies the robot voice that there's a pickup necessary, and no, he won't be on site. The patient will be sedated.

Mr. Freemont's eyes go wide.

Butler hangs up and retrieves a different vial, this one color-coded blue. Mr. Freemont's stomach starts to move, just little twitches for now, signs of the new world clawing to be born. Butler administers the sedative and leaves.

AFTER A TERSE PICKUP at a motel on the edge of town and a quiet drive, Butler leads the officer into his house. The officer said his name on the way over but it isn't sticking. Doesn't need to. He's *the officer*, a position in a system, a hinge. A lever.

Sometimes tools have names, but they don't need them. Especially for the off-the-record freelance work White said the officer's militia connections would make him perfect for.

Butler opens the door a touch harder than necessary and tweaks the jack connection in his skull. The itching flares back up and runs around his skull before settling back down again and going to sleep. He takes a moment to make sure his new sight is still intact, masks it by holding the door for the officer.

The officer takes a seat at the card table Butler's moved into the living room. He looks at the table, the folding chair, the otherwise empty room and folds his hands on the rough plastic tabletop.

And waits patiently for Butler to speak.

A move technically signaling respect but carrying a challenge, too: go on, call the play.

Useful for asserting oneself in a bullpen, but also a sign he doesn't have to hear his own voice.

"The attack. We haven't identified the perpetrators."

"We have identified one. A dropout from the university, working as a typist, I believe."

"Apprehended?"

The officer pauses a second, leave the *as you know* silent. "No, she hasn't been."

"Do we have any more information?"

"She appears to have been in the records as a patient of a research institute on campus, but there are no specifics."

"Not yet?"

The officer shrugs. "Not ever, as it stands. Medical records are behind a wall. It's not impenetrable, but we would need to have something we could put on paper, that the hospital could pull out and show ten, fifteen years from now."

"And we don't have that."

"And it's not likely we'll get it."

Butler nods, pretends to be considering. "I suppose you

wouldn't be surprised if I suggested there was something more happening here."

"No." No pause at all this time.

"What did our mutual friend tell you?"

"He asked me a question. Wanted to know if I could work quietly. I said I could."

"Perfect. There is a group behind the attack on the campus building, and the owners of several sensitive projects in the building would like them apprehended without publicity."

Butler waits. The officer doesn't ask what kind of project, so Butler doesn't have to get grandly allusive. It wouldn't be too hard to play the national-security angle, or the corporate-espionage one. Who knows what goes on in those privately funded campus buildings, after all.

"I assume you have a group of men you can trust?"

BUTLER FEELS BETTER with a few uniforms with him, even if they're out of uniform. The hard way the men hold themselves is the backdrop he needed, the cover to lower his voice and let them be the big stick.

So of course this house is empty.

Butler's cops disperse down the street when he comes back to the front door with the two who helped him enter and gives a signal. They don't quite transform into civilians, can't quite fake that general disinterest, but it's close enough.

Butler goes back into the house and walks room-to-room a little slower than before. This is the second patient who has been missing when they arrived. The first was a four-bedroom, puddle of blood in the middle of the living-room floor, roommates coming in with groceries and beer as they left.

The badges Butler's cops flashed got them out of there but eventually the roommates will wonder why no one's come back there to check up on the case, do whatever college kids expect cops to do.

By that time Butler's cleaning up should be done. Then his lead officer will be able to put together an official explanation for them, make sure that the paperwork all looks like it holds water.

But that doesn't leave them infinite time, and Butler was sure that this patient would be home.

He walks to the middle of the living room, turns around in a circle. His computer vision tells him that there is a heavy presence here, and recent. Immediate. It burns and glows.

But the house is empty.

The traces coming in through the front door don't tell him much. It's the only way into the apartment, so the patient would have had to use it all the time.

Unless the blood on the floor isn't from an abduction. Unless this patient was already feeling ill, his body beginning to change in ways he couldn't understand.

In that case he wouldn't have been using the front door much at all.

Butler turns and walks out, waves his lead officer over. "The patient has been taken by a group of people. They were here recently. Recently enough that their presence was easy to mistake for his."

"You said you could track the infected."

"Yes." Butler meets the officer's eyes. "We are dealing

with a gang of the infected. Most likely they're behind the attack on the campus Institute."

The office whistles through his teeth. "Where to next?"

"We continue identifying and detaining infected. But we move quickly. They may have already been recruited."

Butler get in his car, and pulls away, watches in his rearview to make sure the two unmarked cop cars follow him onto the main street. The officers wanted to take the lead and tail, have him safely in the middle, but it's easier for Butler to see where they need to go if he's not trying to translate it through the radio, and this way there's no gap between him issuing a direction and its execution.

Butler follows the trail out toward downtown. An old house carved into a duplex, the chain link fence around the lot sporting a strip down the middle, making two narrow backyards. Butler parks right in front and gets out, knocks on the door before the officers are out of their cars.

An older man opens the door. He has the kind of mustache his generation was the last to manage hanging off a gaunt square face.

Butler clears his throat. "I'm sorry to intrude, sir."

"The guy from the plasma place, right?"

"Yes. How are you feeling?"

"What in the world did you do to me?"

"No, nothing. Of course we run blood work, though. We run tests. Can we talk?'

The man blink at the answer this isn't, then gives up. Shrugs away from the door, makes for his couch, and Butler has his hand inside his bag.

It's going to take too long, though. This is all going to take too long. All these niceties. Someone's already beaten him to two patients, and the sedated gap between Butler's exit and the Institute pickup would put him in an impossible bind; wait and guard this one, maybe give them time to get to the next. That Katherine fuckup, gathering all her castoff kin to herself, to do who knows what, spreading and mutating in ways he can't monitor.

That changes the entire scope of his mission.

He pushes his hand past the syringes of sedative and finds the little spear-shaped attachment, screws it into the computer his own cable's plugged into.

This isn't a salvage operation anymore, it's a controlled burn to stop a wildfire.

The man gets near his chair and Butler puts one hand helpfully on his back and with the other drives the spear into the base of the man's neck.

There's a quick jerk of the man turning to fight and freezing. Butler holds the spear in place. The man makes a scratching sound, heaves a long ragged breath and makes the scratching sound again.

Something inside the man's body twitches. It waits, twitches again, and starts to thrash.

Butler's connection fizzes and pops. His new vision blanks out, then his regular vision, and he's standing blind, plugging into this man like a broken VCR, but he hears a massive retching and the man falls and pulls Butler with him, atop him. Butler's sight comes back, looking over the back of the man's head, blood and thin toxic-green ichor spraying the carpet and the base of the couch.

The call he makes is for cleanup, not recovery.

At the door, his second stares.

"He almost got me," Butler says. Eases the officer back outside and closes the door.

The officer looks himself over. He's not bleeding from anywhere visible. "And me?"

Butler already knows the man is clear, turns his

augmented sight on him anyway, to be sure. "No. one of them would have had to...inject you, essentially. It's like an infection."

"But if they did."

"It's an infection. You would begin to turn into something."

"Fucking zombie, eh? The walking dead?"

"No, like mushrooms. Have you ever seen those mushrooms they have up in the national forest?"

Blank stare.

"They're just one big creature. A giant fungus, mostly underground, with parts poking up into the air. They look like individual fungi, but they're part of the same big nasty blob. These people we're looking for are all on their way to turning into one of the mushrooms."

EIGHT

THEIR NUMBERS HAVE INCREASED. IT TOOK A WHILE,
some lobbying from Katherine to convince Dani to go out
and look, but a couple of days' worth of that plus their feelings growing more intwined and Dani agreed that they
should pursue what Katherine had always been vaguely
aware of, what Dani can't really ignore anymore.

The feeling of more people like them. Like Katherine.
People who had been hooked into this thing without their
knowledge and find themselves transforming.

The first one was out back of a bar, probably trying to
drink off whatever she was feeling, but it didn't work and
she was sitting on her heels, swaying back and forth when
Dani found her.

The second was at work, trying to interpret some
customer's sandwich order while a manager made the tran-
sition from yelling from the back office to a more in-his-face
sort of aggression. Dani begged off on his behalf, said he had
an appointment.

His job won't be there the next day, but that's the least
of his worries.

Another rescue from an auto shop, a kid who was working the counter but had a dirty rag in his back pocket, too, and Katherine finally tipped her hand, showed what she had in mind.

The new people joined them, their descent arrested and getting to know each other in a visceral kind of way.

Dani's willing to admit that it's helpful, it was the right call, even if their own connection hadn't started to feel stronger with the added fuel of new minds. It's a deeper connection, somehow, and they spend some time navigating that before Dani's cell phone rings from the other room.

Everyone looks at each other, trying to figure out what that noise is.

The sandwich-shop guy figures it out first and points. Dani gets up and hears Mitch in her ear, something about the campus cops and whether everyone's okay.

Dani listens until there's a chance to give him an address.

MITCH TAKES it better than Dani expected, or maybe worse. He's very quiet. Looks at Cora and the rest and doesn't seem all that surprised, but doesn't seem steady, either, walking back out to the front room. He stares out the tinted front window, at the cars jockeying for position at the confusing intersection. Dani goes with him.

"They kept me in like university jail," he says. "I don't know. Campus police department."

"What?"

"I was poking around campus, you know. Trying to see

if there's anything I could find, anybody I used to know. Old friend from the union, maybe a guy I used to know."

"How'd that go?"

Mitch bursts out laughing, looks surprised about it. "Fucking poorly, man. You know I don't think they trust me?"

"The cops or your old friends?"

"The latter. Well. Both." He puts his forehead to the glass. "I'm surprised I'm still trespassed, you know? Would have thought they'd forgotten about me."

"Maybe you just gave them a chance to try out their training."

"Something happened. There were a bunch of people coming and going, and all of a sudden they moved me to the city cop shop and they're filing charges but they kicked me loose. Felony. I don't know, it's over the top. They're fishing."

Doesn't have to say that the bigger fish are all here.

But he's sure he wasn't followed. Maybe they just want to keep him in town. And Dani has to get Katherine ready to go visiting.

She finds Katherine waiting by the back-room door. Standing with all her weight on her heels, hips thrust forward and shoulders forward to match, chest caved back, thick ropes of blood-black mucous stringing down from her chest to her waist. It's better than it has been but there's not much chance of her walking the street unnoticed.

Dani goes over to try to talk Katherine into standing up straighter. She can't quite make her body do it.

They're done debating the outreach angle. Dani has agreed, swallowed down some grave misgivings about taking Katherine with them instead of being guided mentally from the pawn shop. Looking at Katherine doing her best to stand, the swallowing's getting a little harder.

But they are in a pawn shop.

Dani gets Mitch to help look for anything that might make blending easier. Mitch finds a cape in the corner of the shop, a relic from the goth resurgence that even had its own bar for a spell a couple years ago, liquor in beakers and test tubes and heavy boots clomping to medieval computer beats. Heavy black fabric lined with red velvet, waiting for the next revival.

Dani eyes it when Mitch picks it up, thinking it's pretty far from his lane, but he hooks his head over to Katherine, and Dani lets out the first syllable of a harsh laugh.

Mitch grins at her with his eyes, holds his palms out like, hey, give him a chance. Katherine goes to him without any of the sneer Dani would have expected before, lets him twirl the cape around her shoulder and cinch the neck ties up to her throat. The cape falls back and open, dangles from her neck, a flapping red flag.

The arms take a minute. The cape has slits cut midway down, so the arms can poke through when they're at rest, a path to tucking hands into jeans pockets while posing down. Mitch gets Katherine's first arm through easy enough, just hooks the slit over where her arm's hanging, but she has the other wrist pressed to the side of her leg as a counterbalance. Mitch tugs on that hand. Katherine's chest wobbles over too far in the other direction and Dani dives in.

Mitch has already caught her, though, levered his shoulder down to take the weight under the armpit. Dani lifts her up. Mitch's shirt follows for a second, peels free and rests damp on his shoulder.

His eyes get big but he doesn't look at the residue.

IT'S NOT until they're on the road that the weirdness of it all hits Mitch. Back at the pawn shop, it was like seeing old friends after a long time, when they've maybe taken a turn for the eccentric, started wearing bizarre clothes and lost too much weight, but out in the Palm Gulf sun, with the regular grind of pedestrians and cars all around, it doesn't seem that way anymore.

Dani drives. Katherine rides shotgun. Mitch watches them from the back, the way they talk sometimes, just nod in the same direction others. They can hear each other somehow. Dani told him but it's different to see it.

Cora is back at the shop with her new friends. Mitch didn't take more than a quick look and he didn't recognize her. Katherine had to tell him who she was.

The five new people, who Dani called the rescues, they're not in a state to do much of anything yet.

Dani and Katherine navigate in their spooky way to an apartment complex near campus. The lot has a tiny corner of visitor spaces, one barely open with an Explorer parked over the line, taking up a third of it. Dani threads the needle as best she can. Takes out their own sideview mirror and a chunk of the Explorer's paint job but winds up parked more or less legally.

Dani gets out and Mitch slides across the back seat and does the same. Katherine's wedged up against the Ford, has to twist herself around to get out through the little gap the door makes.

Mitch can't watch her for long. It looks like she's about to twist in two.

Katherine rights herself, pulls the cloak tight. Drags the old-fashioned walking stick after her through the car door, grips the big crystal handle and leans against the car door to close it.

He smiles, tries to meet Dani's eyes about how bizarre it is to see her dressed like this, like some goth rocker's daughter playing dress-up in his clothes, but she's looking past him, at one of the units in the complex.

Mitch steps aside, follows them into the courtyard.

Katherine and Dani lead the way right to a door on the ground floor, just past a picnic table with cigarette butts jammed into the hole where an umbrella might go until a dome has formed, melted with the rain into a stinking tar-and-mildew mass. Mitch watches the butts like they're a threat while Dani knocks on the door.

No one answers. Dani knocks again. They all listen in the empty courtyard, and Mitch feels increasingly like he shouldn't be there. He has the physical sense that he's aged out of this place and anyone who caught a look at him would know.

Dani puts her ear to the door and reaches down to try the knob. It turns in her hand. She looks to Katherine. Mitch gets ready with his two cents, his new idea about getting the fuck back to the car, but they don't check with him, just push the door open and expect he'll follow.

There's a single light on inside, deep back toward the rear window that must look out on the parking lot. Four miniature hallways, really just deep doorways, leading to the bedrooms, an open bathroom door between each set. Two couches at an angle facing a television a little too big for the end table it's set on.

Dani and Katherine look to each of the bedroom doors, then the couch. The one they can see the surface of is empty, and to Mitch it looks just like an empty student apartment but they creep forward carefully and Mitch decides to follow suit.

A young man splayed on the second couch, one foot up on the backrest but hidden by the cushion it's jammed under. Face going so pale it's blue, a little bit of blood on the finger of the hand he's pressing over his eyes.

"Hey," Dani whispers.

"Y'all," the kid moans, barely audible, "just gimme a while, okay? I thought you were going out."

"We weren't," Katherine says.

The kid jumps and Mitch can tell from most of a room away that he's not right. He can't move the way he wants to but isn't used to it yet. Like his bones hurt.

"I don't know you."

"No," Dani says. "We think...I think someone's done something to you."

He clutches his fingers at the spaces in his ribcage.

"We can help you, maybe."

THEY KEEP GROWING. Three new people huddle off to the side of the front room, in a semicircle around Katherine. Her creature sits on her lap, one narrow limb slipped into the skin of each new person. It doesn't seem to need to puncture Katherine's body anymore, has that connection stabilized and reliable.

Mitch watches them. Imagines for the dozenth time

going home, putting his feet up on the coffee table and waiting to fall asleep on the couch, to wake up in a world that makes sense.

But that world is gone, already feels a little foreign, and it's time to get used to what's happening.

He walks over until he's standing just outside the circle. No one acknowledges him. He's wearing short sleeves but rolls them up anyway, Ponyboy Curtises them past his shoulders, and sits.

Katherine leans toward him so her creature can get a better angle and he grits his teeth until the point slips in, and he doesn't feel anything, has to look down to see that it has really penetrated his skin, and then he only has a minute for his skin to prickle in that vomit kind of way before his brain goes white.

Every muscle in his body twitches itself stiff. Something enters him and tears its way up his arm.

When he comes around the others are gone, Katherine's gone, and Dani sits against the wall with him.

Mitch rubs the inside of his arm. He'd expected it to hurt, and it did, the breaking of the skin getting lost in the dagger rush up and down his arms, carving into his shoulder and spearing his fingertips from the inside. It hurt, but the pain accumulated enough of itself that it became something else entirely. From a violation of his body and the reactions of his nerves to a final rupture in some internal wall he hadn't known existed, boundaries clarified and shattered by the pain.

There's something behind the rubble of the walls, but he can't make sense of it yet. It sounds like voices, but without words. His attention gets tugged in different directions by the different voices. They move and swell but circle a point far below. A mass of echoes. Not one thing, not merged entirely, but connected.

The sounds enter his body, reverberate through his broken-wider mind. He recognizes them not by sound but by feel.

"It's a lot, huh?" Dani whispers. Loud enough to shake his fillings. "Entry has gotten harder."

"Harder?"

"Since there were fewer people swimming around down there. Close up, at least."

It takes Mitch a moment to see what she means, but there's more echoing further away. Hard to feel, darker. Slower. But there.

Cold murmuring. A rising numbness.

Dani grips his shoulder just as his breath begins to catch. "Careful. We can't get too close to them."

He opens his mouth to ask how she knew he was doing just that, but of course. She can feel what's coming off him as well as he can her. Better.

"They're not people?"

"They are. Or they were. It doesn't seem like they're communicative, just a draw. A trap."

Mitch wonders how close Cora is to that category.

Dani does too.

"We're heading out again," she says instead. "Do you feel up to it?"

"I think so."

"It feels more like everyone else has become you than the other way around. Anyway, it'll be good to get out into the world, moving around."

So he follows her to the car. He gets in back with one of the new people, a tall man in his fifties whose name he doesn't know but whose thoughts he can feel. Katherine sits

147

shotgun, creature in her lap, and Dani just gets the keys in the ignition before Katherine notices something.

The door to the pawn shop opens.

Cora stands just inside.

Dani hops out of the car, waving at Cora to get back, and Cora does, but it's to make way for another figure, walking slowly and wrapped in two layers of sweaters, hood up and face down.

One of Cora's bodyguards.

The pawn shop door drifts closed and what might still be a person takes a long time to walk to the car. Mitch looks around at the traffic, all those car windows glinting in the sun. Cora's friend looks normal enough until they get closer. The sleeves of their sweater are already starting to cling at the wrists, setting in semisolid skin.

They stop at the door. Mitch can feel Dani doesn't want to let them in. Mitch agrees and not only because they're standing by his door and he'll wind up in the middle, closer contact than he's ready for. But his new acquaintance isn't taking the hint, isn't going back in the shop, is just standing there in broad daylight, so Mitch pops his door and scoots over.

Cora's friend squishes into the seat and Mitch waits a moment, then reaches over their lap to slam the car door. A sweet smell fills the car, like flowers and soil, but there's something under it and on second breath it's suffocating. Beyond rot, a level of decomposition not possible in nature. Acetone and lemon and rendered chicken fat.

But there's a sturdy focus to their mind. Mitch feels it, below the thoughts of his friends and less formed, but coiled and ready for violence.

Mitch wonders if Cora felt something coming, something they can't pick up on, and sent some help.

Katherine agrees.

Dani pulls out of the lot.

DANI FEELS something amiss as soon as she gets out of the car. She tries to keep it from the others at first, doesn't want Mitch to catch wind and lose his cool, but he feels it immediately. Katherine does too.

Beneath the musty motor-oil scent of coiling heat and coming rain, the skin-and-blood tang of too many people on this block, none of them visible.

Katherine moves first, fast wobbling strides toward the house, one arm cupped around her creature under her cloak. Walking stick tapping heavily, adjusting her course.

Two men emerge from behind the house next door.

Katherine knows because Dani sees them, but she doesn't change direction. The men reach her quickly. One of them grabs her by the shoulders and spins her around. The other gets behind her, handcuffs in hand.

Katherine lifts her hands over her head and faces the first man. Six of her creature's arms lance through the fabric of her cloak and jerk the top half of her torso forward and thwack their way into the man's skin.

Pops of blood, little bursts. None of the smooth clean piercing from the pawn shop here, just old-fashioned ragged stabbing.

Katherine's face is still upright, the same angle as if she were standing up straight. She stares at the man's chest.

And looks up to his eyes.

The man dry-gulps and staggers backward. He reaches

for his gun when he should be reaching to break his fall. His head smacks the sidewalk.

The creature's limbs pull it after him, Katherine after it. The second man holds onto her shoulder and follows them down.

The stabbed man goes limp.

Dani is startled to see Mitch running toward Katherine before she does, black tee shirt and a trickle of blood down one arm. She slams the door and gets around the front bumper and the windshield bursts into a spiderweb before a booming snap.

Dani drops to the ground and covers her head. The back door slams. Cora's guard walks past Dani, toward the gunfire.

The sky tears open and sheets of gray rain roar. Flash puddles gathering and spattering on the asphalt.

Another gunshot, duller in the downpour. A chunk of flesh splashes down, taints the water around it on contact.

Dani flinches back but Cora's guard is still standing. Not even swaying. Yellow pus oozing from a shoulder exit wound.

Two more tear open, yellow sunbursts in time with two more reports. Cora's guard absorbs the impact. Drops to their knees just long enough to give the impression of succumbing, then pushes off from the ground and charges impossibly fast. Gawky, like running in wedges, but straight and with no uncertainty about where the shots are coming from.

The shooter gets one more off but it goes wide. Cora's guard plunges their hands into a bush and gets a suit jacket and a fistful of hair and doesn't slow a bit, yanks the man from his crouch. He drops his gun. Gummy fingers rake across his throat, leaving wide smears of dull purple joined by fresh bright blood.

The two fleshes become one, and Dani can't quite tell where the boundary is, but only one of them bleeds.

And she almost looks away, doesn't want to be watching this at all, but feels something of a duty to keep her eyes on it, to witness.

The shooter's neck comes all the way open now, pink rubbery tissue and mushy red meat, streaming down the street in the rain.

Dani's muscles start itching, watching this, the way a leg on a plane might when the owner realizes they're no more than halfway through their flight, but her whole body. Soreness and the twitch for movement, for release, and a doubt that physical exertion will be enough.

She rolls away from the car and scrambles toward Mitch and Katherine on all fours. Katherine still leans over one of the men, though her creature has come free from the cape and works its limbs between his ribs in full glinting view of the world.

His mouth is open. He might be screaming.

Mitch and the other man both have their hands on the grip of a pistol. The struggle for it must have been close at first, but now the man's got his legs on either side of Mitch's stomach, pinning him down, and the gun is slowly turning. Dani shoves her palms against the blacktop hard enough to work up to her feet in stride. She runs across the grass strip and the sidewalk onto the lawn and drops her shoulder, drives it into the soft patch above the man's hip.

The gun fires once. Mitch claps his hands to his ears. The man drops the gun by Mitch's head and rolls over, reaching for his kidney.

Mitch's hands scrabble around. Find the gun. He sits up

with it, face scrunching up to try to dim the ringing, and Dani crawls through the wet grass until she can pull herself up the wood steps to her feet and to the front door.

It's not the first impression she hoped they'd make, but the person in the house has been exposed. Katherine felt it, and this armed greeting party confirms it. They need to get whoever it is out of here intact.

When another shot goes off, she only looks back long enough to check that Mitch is on the winning side of it. She pounds on the door. Shouting from inside, about go away or leave her alone or something, and Dani tries to explain but there's too much noise and the yelling inside hasn't stopped. She puts her shoulder to the wood and the latch gives easy, no bolt.

It's an old house, maintained a bit but never renovated, and Dani shrugs past a too-steep stairway and through something like an entryway into a living room with a couple doors coming off it.

It's just a television on a nightstand and a corporate-surplus sort of sofa, a woman in pajamas sitting on top of her legs on the far side, clutching a chef's knife with both hands.

Dani backs up a step, thinks better of remaining in view of the doorway. Steps into the shadow of the staircase, holds her hands up.

"There's something wrong with you."

The woman straightens the blade, aims the point at Dani and sights down its length.

"No, I mean...you haven't felt right. I imagine not for a while."

The woman doesn't speak.

"We can help you, but we have to go now. There will be more of them coming."

The woman keeps her knife as she gets up, but she walks in front of Dani, too.

She pauses in the doorway before pushing ahead at a trot. Dani follows. The carnage hits her eyes fresh. Three bodies in varying states of deconstruction, a blown-out skull and a raggedly perforated chest and a gouged throat.

Rain making a scarlet slick of the street.

The crew piling into the car, now that they've seen Dani emerge from the house. Looking every bit the killers.

The woman must have doubts but she's cast her lot. Dani silently promises to make it worth it, and as they pile in, the woman half in Dani's lap in the front seat, trying to make sense of that smell, a van turns onto the street from one direction, white panels and dark windows, and a man walks from the other.

Soaked-through white coat and a steel briefcase, blood smeared up one side of his face. Cord running from his neck, and the second he's in view something turns over in all their brains but the new recruit's, and the world goes dead all around this man. They can't see his features but he carries the void with him, has come to absorb everything he can.

And Dani's blood is still itching, still pumping differently. She feels that the others feel it too. The next part of their change has started, and Dani hopes it's triggered by movement, by conscious action or just plain time, and not mere bloodshed.

Something in the rush of violence has changed her, is changing all of them.

She struggles the car into gear and whips it around, hydroplanes toward the opposite end of the street from the van and the computer man.

THE PAWN SHOP air is thicker now, with everyone scurrying around, searching for anything useful they can reappropriate from the shelves and stirring up the dust. The ringing in their blood hasn't stopped since the violence broke out at the last house and they can feel themselves changing faster.

They're up to seven new people, plus Dani and Katherine and Mitch and Cora and her three guards. It's a crew that would soon enough need a new place to stay, or a second one, but that problem was at least a few visits down the road, and they could have taken their time about it a little.

But the phlebotomist apparently has a computer plugged into his head to find where they're going to be and a personal cop army to walk behind. The one place he'd be guaranteed to have a shot at all of them together is here.

So they're looking for supplies and they're thinking. There's not much useful except for some clothes, scarves and hats to hide their faces. A few knives, a set of hunting and camping blades in particular, and a handful of guns. The guns are under a locked plexiglas case, though, and the lock won't give. Danie hits it once with a bronze ashtray but it bounces off. Mitch raises his eyebrows at the joke he thinks she's making, but she winds up to swing again, from further back and two-handed, and he just about jumps out of his shoes to get between her and the case.

"It felt like you were joking," he says. Still getting used to how he can sense what's going on in his friend's brain, learning that even this kind of communication has room for gaps.

"Oh, I mean, I thought it would be fun."

Mitch snorts. "Ah, yeah, I get that. But it's alarmed."

"No one's here."

"No, but how do we know?"

And Dani taps the ashtray against her palm, thinking about how if they're getting tracked here anyway, it won't hurt much about the cops.

One of the new people, a onetime petty thief, doesn't think they were cops, exactly, at the last house.

Dani reminds him of the badge Mitch saw clipped to a belt mid-struggle.

Katherine thinks about the phlebotomist, the plain clothes, the opening fire on a residential street in broad daylight.

They leave the guns but pass out the knives.

Mitch winds up with a big one, the kind with an angry notch in the end like a hunter would have. For skinning, he thinks, though he's not real sure about the mechanics of that.

One of the new people is from out in the county, though, and as soon as he thinks it Mitch takes in that muscle memory.

The tingling feeling awoken by the fray at the last house keeps up, urging him to move. Mitch knows Dani is worried that it's more than a reaction to the fight, that it is itself bloodlust, a mounting urge that could take them over, make them the monsters the men in suits think they're hunting. Pure instinct and violence. Walking mounds of muscle and teeth.

It doesn't feel that way to Mitch, feels more like access to new instincts, but if it the rush they're riding is only festering murder he's ready to lean into it, let it clear a path for them.

It could serve them well if they had a direction to point it.

Katherine has the idea first, and there's a quick flutter of discussion before the crew reaches basic agreement

The darkest place in the tornado of voices that aren't voices murmuring down below, the blind eye in the middle of the city Dani warned him about. The one place they all take for granted they would never have good enough reason to go, such that their collective mental map of the city doesn't really include it.

Whatever's happening above ground, it has its roots beneath.

Dani raises the issue of the others, the new people they've only just begun pulling from the whirlpool of mutation. Wouldn't this be leaving them outside to fend for themselves?

Mitch has an idea, though, and it's out into the group brain before he's thought it all the way through: the center of their operation would have some kind of control, some system for tracking and measuring, a way for the people responsible to monitor things.

And, Katherine adds, a crisis at the center would draw forces from the periphery. They would have every gun the program has at its disposal converging on them under the campus.

Which, no, that's not exactly what they've been hoping for so far.

But it would at least buy the others some time.

They've all heard the screams, after all. Felt the new minds reach out and stop. They know what Butler's up to, even if they haven't seen a corpse yet.

They pile into Dani's car and the pickup truck the new person who was once a mechanic owns and head toward campus.

KATHERINE'S CREATURE adjusts itself in her lap, jabbing limbs into the flesh of her legs. It's gotten more comfortable with vehicles, but it still gets agitated. Katherine runs her hands along its carapace, stares out the window like she can protect them by sheer attention.

At least her creature's on edge too.

They weave toward campus, heading south until they can cross under the pedestrian overpass, where there's less traffic.

Mitch is trying out different grips on his knife in the back seat. Trying to make himself feel dangerous. She trusts him, but the way he moves is so fleshy, so still-human, that she's not sure how useful he'll be in another fight. Everyone's still acclimating.

They're doing it faster, becoming more like her since the scene at the last house, but it might not be enough.

They speed to a turnoff, barely visible through the bushes and the concrete half-wall with the Fightin' Turtle crest. Down into a basement-level loading dock, like a hidden concrete room. Empty.

They've all been expecting to find resistance before now, but the building seems empty by regular campus standards, let alone any kind of increased security.

Like maybe the Institute has started to clear itself out.

They pile out of the cars and the door to the loading

dock ratchets open for four men, moving with an urgency that seems more surprised than prepared.

They all wear dark coveralls and sunglasses, walkie-talkies and gun belts. Automatic rifles of wildly different shapes in their hand.

The men unload. Pop of a riot gun, then the booming rattle of live ammunition reverberating off the concrete. Everyone dives behind the truck but bullets find skin. Impossible to tell whose, to isolate the source of sudden pain. Blood mingling on the concrete. A baton round catches Mitch in the head, crunches skull above his eye. Burst of blood and bone, and he staggers and spins but doesn't fall.

Katherine twists around and slings her creature bowling-ball-style. It draws fire in the air but isn't hit, stretches out its limbs and lands on the rear window of the truck, pointed limbs dimpling the safety glass, and bounds back onto the side of one man's head. Two points into the neck, deep and then out. Twin gouts of blood. The creature takes a rickety ride down with the body.

The crossfire follows the creature down and cuts a second man apart.

Two left.

Watching their companion bleed out from friendly fire makes them hesitant. Cora's crew moves before they can recover, less tackling then colliding with one of them, coming down with forearms and knees until his jaw cracks against the asphalt.

Mitch looks up. Still standing. Rolls his head in circles, head swelling.

Katherine reaches out for her creature, lets it crawl up her arm like a friendly tarantula.

The newcomers surround the last man and take his gun

away and brace to tear him apart, but Katherine holds out her hands.

"Stop," speaking out loud because she's not sure how well they hear her yet. "Let's keep one alive."

And the creature follows her lead, puts its other limb-points slowly into his neck and shoulders and chest. The man collapses. Katherine gets her hands under the man's legs, doesn't have the leverage in her anymore but gets the others to grab him and hoist him up.

He starts to turn, but too fast, too forced. His brain hemorrhages what he knows into theirs but it's hard to interpret, and he doesn't seem to have ever been in the basement.

The people in the basement are definitely gone, though, have been moving their equipment out for days.

Mitch stares straight ahead through his good eye. If he hasn't already lost the other, he soon will, and he should be wailing or in a coma but something is carrying him along.

Dani presses her hand to her stomach, holding in blood or something even more vital.

And several of the newcomers leak from wounds they don't seem to have noticed yet.

Katherine thinks the momentum of the group, something about their growing bond along with their ongoing mutation is working on them, making them harder to kill.

It's more than adrenaline, but here they are, and the door leading inside is open.

They link arms and lean, carry each other inside in a gaping huddle. Some of them must be dead but they don't seem to be. All the voices are accounted for.

The stairwell Cora once emerged from is locked, push-bar fixed rigid.

Their auto shop employee knows how locks work,

though, and goes to rummage through some classrooms until he finds a box of paperclips.

Katherine remembers thinking that she should have gotten a little bit more creative in her approach to paying rent when she was working at SpeakScript.

Maybe it's her imagination, but she feels like she gets a little reaction from Cora. A cold nudge in the back of her mind along the lines of a raised eyebrow.

The world kind of slows down, just for a moment, to make room for the connection Katherine thought was gone forever.

And the lock springs open.

Cora walks right to the front, brings her entourage with her. Katherine pulls her cape tighter and follows, lifting her creature up to perch on her shoulder like an eldritch parrot. Stands as close behind Cora as she can, puts her hand on her back to keep close.

And they descend into the Institute.

THE HALLWAYS ARE IDENTICAL. Some kind of optical illusion gray-on-gray pattern that makes intersections hard to see, directions difficult to remember. Dani had expected a sinister concrete sort of deal, harsh lights and vile puddles, but instead it feels like an outer space basement den.

The place seems entirely empty. She can't feel anyone here, affected or not.

Dani puts her hand to the wall and reaches, can't sense anyone outside the basement at all, either. This is a mute bubble.

She can't stop sensing it, though, the cut-off-ness that's no different, really, from what was most of her life. Now it rings, an angry absence surrounding the basement lab. This is the heart of the enemy, protected from their minds.

The crew sweeps the floor. It's only the one level, as far as they can tell. They find a series of holding rooms with steel doors and bright white walls inside, medical tables and a camera and speaker in the corner of the ceiling. An observation room across the hall, most of it cleaned out in a hurry.

The first occupied room they find isn't promising. Dani shoves the door open with her foot and finds most of a person strapped to the bed. He's not moving, has gone thin enough that the wrist straps hardly seem tight enough to do their jobs.

Dani creeps forward until she's sure the man isn't going to move. She looks at his face and jumps hard enough to almost lose her balance when his eyes, frozen wide, whip around in his skull, chasing the sound of her.

Dani scrambles back toward the door to the room, finally collides with a squish. Looks up, and it's one of Cora's. Shocking relief. Dani edges around Cora's friend and watches them walk to the prisoner.

Maybe the two of them have enough in common that they can help.

They start to find prisoners faster now. The lab only had time to evacuate the rooms near the center. That includes what looks like their records room and a cluster of offices, but only a handful of the holding rooms.

A clump of the crew find a different kind of door. Feel the screaming gulf deep underneath their mental connection is behind it.

Dani watches Katherine go in and tries to follow but Katherine wants the room alone.

She gathers the others to continue on.

KATHERINE CROSSES her legs and sits, bends forward until she can put her elbows on the floor, her chin in her hands. This room is important, takes up most of this block of hallway and far enough up that there must be room carved into the guts of the building itself, between classrooms and offices. She feels something behind the massive glass wall.

Katherine calls her creature and the clicking footsteps pause on the threshold. It knows to be cautious here. It comes in, though, creeps just past Katherine's elbows.

Something in the tank stirs. Her creature reaches out a pointy leg and taps. The stirring kicks and recedes. Katherine stretches a finger out toward the glass, into the cold air coming off the case, and the void rushes toward her, swirls and clenches frustrated against the glass.

Black tendrils like cursed egg whites whisping off a central mass that doesn't bounce enough light to be visible, straining into a sickening green where it twists over itself.

It's only there for a second, and she's left holding her finger in the air.

She feels something, though. Like a wind through her private thoughts.

No one else reacts. Katherine looks around, sees the rest of the crew waiting outside the door.

She scoots forward on knees and elbows. Feels the layer of icy air around the glass. Looks as deep into the dark as she can but can't see anything. It's all just darkness in there, condensation from her breath clouding it all over.

She pushes the pad of her finger to the glass, flinches at the cold but doesn't move, and the being inside rushes forward.

It swirls around her finger. She wonders how many people have ever gotten this good a look for this long, feels the cold starting to eat at the skin of her finger.

The specimen in the case would be hard to take in even if it did sit still. It's massive, larger than the building above looks from the outside, and it moves counterclockwise, gathering itself and striking at the glass and gathering again. Something like a slug sloughing off layers of itself to make gossamer arms, an absence except where those arms get thin or the mass of it folds in over itself.

It's the source of what happened, of course. Her creature knows this, has slowly retraced its steps until it's behind her, perfectly aware that it is itself a deviation from the source.

But if there's a connection Katherine can't understand it. She feels static and a deep riptide pull.

When Katherine pulls her finger away and lets the creature zip back into the depths of its tank and looks back, Cora's there behind the others, beaming on the edge of violence.

Katherine's felt the emotion before, though it's strange here. It's like the puffing-up every man seems to know how to do in a confrontation people are watching. It's a protective flex.

Katherine settles back on her arms and watches the depths. Her finger burns. She shakes it in the air, slips the tip through her makeshift bandages and tucks it inside her chest cavity, pressing up against the half-scabbed chest wall.

Deep inside the case, nothing much happens. Maybe an occasional kick, repositioning, but the glass seems plenty strong and Katherine is content to sit, watching, with Cora and company at her back.

ANOTHER DOOR OPENS onto another hallway. It doesn't seem possible. The lab resists mental maps, fights against the brain like a haunted hotel. Some combination of the paneling being disorienting as well as soundproof and the twisting hallways.

The new hall is a straight shot to one door. Dani and two others stalk down it.

They push the door open on a silent hive.

A row of tables running along each wall toward the back, a double row down the middle. A person on each table. Two large computer banks at the back of the room sprout cables out to the bodies on each table.

It's like a massive open-air office with people on the tables instead of monitors. Dani looks around, feels her posture change walking in. A silent SpeakScript, a part-time contractor office job where they don't have to let you go home.

The bodies strapped to the tables don't move, but she can feel that they're alive. She reaches out to one of them, holds her hand over the dull flesh, the startlingly white and open eyes. She senses something but can't see thoughts. The mind of these people are locked away, underwater.

She calls for Cora and retreats to the doorway with the other two. Cora's coming, but she still moves slow. They wait, standing still for the first time since arriving in the lab. The size of the building comes into focus, the tons of concrete and steel piled atop them.

Dani starts to lift off from her body, from their collective body. Either she's more claustrophobic than she thought or someone with her is.

The door opens and Cora fills it. Dani comes back down. Cora walks slowly down the aisle.

Dani realizes this is the first time she's seen Cora move alone since she broke out. Her three friends have split off.

Cora pauses by a bed and stares down at the face, the protruding ribcage and swollen fingers. Crosses the room to another bed in the middle, not at random. Walks along that way for a while and then traces her way around to the other aisle, the beds on the other side. From there to a bed on the other far wall and down to one of the computer units.

Dani hadn't noticed the wires on the floor, glued down under protective plastic sheaths.

She does now.

Cora finds the cable she wants and notes the beds she paused by. Unplugs the last connection from the computer by sliding a long narrow needle from a rubbery interface on a heavy data jack. The needle is just about invisible in her hand. It might be fear that makes her hesitate, might be the rubicon she's about to cross with no clear idea what's on the other side. But she holds it awhile.

And then sticks it into her arm.

Anxiety whips its way right up Dani's spine and she's half turned and making a run for it before she can isolate the feeling, convince her body it's coming from outside. She's been getting used to believing signals from outside her own meat, though, training her body in exactly the art of accepting freakouts like this, so it doesn't all the way take.

She gets herself under control, turns back into the room quick enough to see a zig-zag of the bodies on the beds lift up and fall back down, twitch a little bit at the ends of their limbs.

Cora's head cocks.

Little bursts of memory coming from her. Coming through her. Mediated for mortal consumption, the source of Dani's sudden fear:

The inside of a plexiglass cube swiss-cheesed with inch-wide holes. Utter darkness. The floor growing brighter and someone screaming and the cube descending into a massive glass case that goes suddenly and violently dark, tendrils of that darkness squeezing up through the holes in the floor.

Then: an ambulance ride diverted. Wheezing for breath, fighting ultimately against the lungs themselves. A stretcher pulled out at the university, a tube hooked up to a giant specimen case. The tube fills with sticky black particles and the lungs seize, then freeze, then start breathing again all wrong.

Then: a quick fix to quiet the shakes, another to numb the nerves. A scalpel peeling off a thick strip of numb flesh, blue gloves laying a steak of putrid black meat on top of the wound. The analgesics work until they don't, until the blood of the subject and the blood of the specimen merge and produce a very permanent shock.

The crew can't breathe, their skins tingling. Long seconds before they come back, their bodies realize the death they just experienced might not have been real, that their organs aren't really shutting down.

Cora pulls the next needle from its rubber home.

A FILM FORMS over Mitch's left eye. He doesn't touch it. Partly doesn't want to know what residue would be on his finger, mostly doesn't want to interfere with it working.

He can feel the dent in his skull. The ocular bone caved in, and he can't see out of that eye, but it doesn't hurt. The eye isn't damaged, he somehow knows, but there's swelling and this new film his body's trying out.

He settles in the room with Katherine. She doesn't mind him coming in, though everyone else who isn't off getting the lay of the land is huddled outside the entrance, giving Katherine her space. He comes in and she doesn't move her eyes from the case, but she says hello. Seems glad to see him.

He feels the same way, tries to let her know.

She gets it. He's getting the hang of this whole thing.

But his balance is off. He can't feel the damage, really, doesn't seem to have a swelling brain or internal bleeding-out, but his coordination is all wrong. Maybe it will come back with time, with the pink film growing over his wound, the change happening in all of them.

But for now he slumps down against the wall, gets his knees inside his arms.

Katherine smiles and for a moment he's here with just an old friend. He feels safe.

Then she asks if he minds if she keeps working. He indicates that he probably won't even notice, but by all means.

Then he gets his first glimpse of the source.

Right away it's clear that they're different. Whatever

else this thing is, part of it is an absence, a sucking negation looking for something to attach itself to.

Katherine's trying to reach it. He feels her reaching out, feels her getting something back but the organism somehow doesn't acknowledge the connection.

Katherine and the monster go back and forth. It fades back, she regroups and calls it. The picture getting clearer with each go-round.

It's all a bit beyond Mitch's range right now. But he watches.

STRANGERS COME DOWN THE HALL. Katherine feels their approach before they get there. It takes some time for all of them to get inside.

When they do, they're a little bit familiar. They're like Cora's guard but worse off, holding each other up where legs and spines can't do it anymore. Skin not the soft desiccation of Cora but something waxier, stretched and easily tearable.

Cora has raised the bodies from that room.

Katherine gets up to let them by but that's not what they're after. The first through the door stand to either side of Katherine. The others fill in behind those two. Katherine settles back down, strained-to-uselessness muscles in her back appreciating this, none-too-gently suggesting that this might come to be her default posture.

The idea of crawling everywhere seems ridiculous and weak, undignified, but then she's seen herself walk through her friends' eyes.

She pushes her knees out and presses her elbows into the floor. Gets herself a couple feet closer to the glass fairly smoothly and with a minimum of pain.

The crowd inches behind her to keep up.

She's not sure what to do now that they're here, so she takes another stab at what she had been doing. Touches the glass, keeps herself from flinching away when the creature comes, just lifts her fingers a half-inch off the surface to keep from burning another.

Finds the gulf down beneath the swirl of thoughts and voices that binds the crew, the nothing corresponding to the mass of freezing chaos in front of her.

Pushes, trying to feel what there is to feel.

But now her reach is further, one layer deeper. She has a boost and a mediator, a room full of them pushing her signal.

Her reach expands and doesn't stop at that. The memories they've all seen from awakening them kick up again, all at the same time, and call up their echo from everybody in the network. The moment they started turning, the events that put them in the plasma clinic, a half-filled-in conversation in a graveyard. More than a few sets of flashing red-and-blue lights.

And from that momentum she gets a push into the much deeper history of the creature in the case.

Deep history, they learn, is unimaginably cold.

PULLED loose from the circuit of research and deployment, data collection and symptom collation, yet rooted and settling into the core of that machinery, the crew reels all at once at the contact with the source.

The newest among them have felt it at least once before, before their catatonia. Directly and incomprehensibly. They became linked into the place itself, part of the machine, providing some kind of human-computer service even as their brains shorted out, their skin thinned.

But they're pulled from that and into a new configuration. Encountering the creature with some more distance.

The rest of the crew is no less agape at the contact. With this deep ancient nothing. Cold hunger and something like inquisitiveness. Searching for the next vector, the next conquest. A cunning animal void.

That section of their collective holding some spiritual convictions finds them sickly mirrored in the feeling; those without any feel a vague religious stirring. Something this ancient isn't god, but it isn't exactly unlike a god, either. And it has remade them.

There's a key difference, though, and it's in how they've removed themselves from its death orbit, reconstituted on new ground. Not yet solid but theirs. This creature is an origin point, yes, but an origin is repulsive when you've moved past it.

Cora in the coma room, four heavy cords hanging from the bio-ports in her arms, exploring the building's network.

Dani and Mitch in the hallway, Mitch's eye covered in a hardening web of dull pink tissue now, regaining its sight if at a different angle, brain still learning to compensate, relying on the eyes of his crew; Dani holding up the body next to her and paying attention to the new way her blood moves.

The others on a stationary patrol, spread enough

through the halls that between them they have a panoramic view of almost the entire space.

But all watching Katherine clutching the floor of the specimen room like a spider, back in two arcs, one hand lifted a little bit, facing the thing head on.

Katherine lifts her finger again but doesn't touch the glass. Points at it instead.

Her creature rams its front limbs through

It's only a small crack but it's enough.

The building howls. Light pours into the case from above, gets mostly swallowed up but also kicks up little rivulets of steam. The monster in there spins faster, less regularly. Starts to thrash around, giving off parts of itself.

Hiss of gas from vents overhead.

Cora forces the steel doors blocking them in from the upper world to close harder than they want to, grinding gears into sparks, and then cuts the power from their motors.

The gas seeping from the vents scalds their skin and everyone crouches down low. Cora tries to remove it but it's slow. Dani feels the hair singe away from the back of her head and then a cooling rush, backup vents hidden in the floor whispering to life.

The first emotion they've felt from Cora: a grim violent triumph as the enemies' gas is forced back up to the surface, back home to them.

And the caged beast whips its way around its enclosure.

It has its urge to assimilate, to merge with the walking now that it finds itself on their turf, replaced by the desperation of survival, but the light and the gas have done their work.

It unfurls part of itself, way deep in the middle of its folds, and shows them a grid of precise slashes, all oozing infection-green, before losing all form, shedding its flesh to the floor in the green dripping sheets.

They leave the room, shut the door for the last time.

Down the hall, Cora expands their mental reach, out into the world somehow, to sense more of them, more of the exposed and affected, the unwillingly becoming, than they had expected.

Their bestial father dead and formless, the crew gets to work.

LATER

Sundays after the farmers' market, the plaza downtown gets quiet early. No kind of outdoor events, with the citizens getting rest for the workweek and classes, no evening show at the theater on the south end of the plaza.

A few blocks south of these, the new parking-lot light the city put in next to the convenience store only a few weeks ago is shards on the asphalt, already mostly scattered away. What's left gleams dull yellow in the old light over the door. It hadn't helped enough to stop people calling the place the Stab-N-Grab. Now it will never have the chance.

At the end of the parking lot, apart from the four dudes drinking out of paper bags and occasionally shoving each other's shoulders, keeping hands in pockets, a thin figure. Dark glasses on at night but the hood down on their sweatshirt. Hair slicked back in thick strands.

No one fucks with them. It's not because they've established that they're dangerous or to be taken seriously. More of a feeling that follows them around, a natural-feeling distance to be maintained.

The advocate stands there, waiting, as every night. Not

always here, but places like it. The edges of parts of town, holes in the municipal map. Sometimes people show up. Sometimes not. There are those who go looking, but that's not the advocate's job.

Their job is to wait, to blend into background and let the people who can feel their presence find them.

A kid approaches the parking lot, keeping to the curb and the shadows. Looks at the advocate for a second, then at the light of the convenience store. Like there's a choice posed here, like those are two equivalent options.

The advocate cocks their eyebrows and waits. Generally refrains from speaking first.

"Hey, do I know you?" the kid says.

"I don't think so."

"Oh. You seem familiar."

"You are sick."

"Hey, fuck, man, fine. I didn't mean anything."

"No. I mean if I seem familiar, I think you might be sick."

They talk awhile more like that, around a subject the kid knows perfectly well. It's not about the words, it's about two voices. It's about establishing communication.

It doesn't always work. But sometimes.

This night, the advocate invites the kid to accompany them to the abandoned bike shop a few blocks away. The kid shrugs, says he's always on the lookout for a good squat, knows that's not exactly what's happening here.

They make the walk in silence, trust already as established as it's likely to be.

The bike shop was a restaurant once, is boarded up now. Empty, dark. The doors are sealed but the board over a window on the side of the building has a little give it to it.

The advocate holds it aside for the kid, who waits for them to go first.

The advocate smiles and obliges.

The kid follows.

Inside, a group of five people sit in a circle. Something shaped like a large spider under a blanket on one of their laps.

"Come in," one of them says. "I think we might be able to help you."

ACKNOWLEDGMENTS

Mark would like to thank:

Kij Johnson, for heroically reading far more drafts of this than could have been healthy or enjoyable;

Giselle Anatol, Phil Drake, Ari Linden, and Paul Scott for their valuable questions and feedback;

Logan Priess, for giving this an early read and for that time we found a copy of *Ninja III: The Domination* in my local video-rental place;

For that matter, Liberty Hall in Lawrence, KS, for having a cool video-rental place and particularly for that one time someone put *Ninja III: The Domination* in the new-releases section with a staff-recommendation sticker on it;

Mom and Dad and Paul for their enthusiasm and support;

And, of course, Caroline, for making with me a life I like living. That time we stayed up way too late talking about Hold Steady lyrics? I feel like that all the time. I still don't want to get out of the car.

ABOUT THE AUTHOR

Mark grew up near Orlando. He lives in Kansas now, where he teaches literature and writing, with his wife and two dogs. This is his second novel. He has an underwhelming internet presence at <u>mutantcircuit.com</u>.

A Small Light & Other Stories - Sara Century

A mysterious woman stalks a seaside town. An isolated couple inhabit a house full of tropical birds. A rowboat floats down a river toward a witch's cave. Death wanders an unnamed city during the plague. Sara Century's debut short story collection carries with it surreal visions inspired by pulp paperbacks, art house films, comic books of all flavors, and classic queer villains.

A Small Light & Other Stories gathers tales that hinge on troubled characters with nothing left to lose encountering existential horrors, where everyday problems escalate into insurmountable monsters, and we find ourselves unable to escape dreams long since transformed into nightmares.

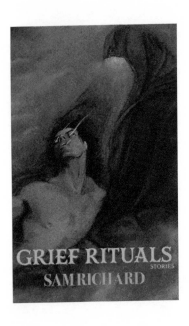

Grief Rituals - Sam Richard

From Wonderland Award-Winning author Sam Richard comes twelve more uncomfortable tales of sorrow, ruination, and transformation.

A young widow joins a spousal loss support group with bizarre methods of healing. An aging punk is stalked by something ancient and familiar in the labyrinthian halls of an art complex. A couple renting out a small movie theater are interrupted by a corrosive force of nature. Through these stories of weird horror and visceral sorrow, Richard shows us ways grief can be transcendent—but only if we know which rituals to practice.

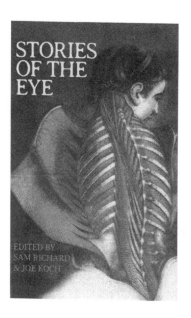

Stories of the Eye edited by Sam Richard & Joe Koch

An anthology of horror stories exploring the relationships between artists and their subjects. Featuring stories from Andrew Wilmot, M. Lopes da Silva, Gwendolyn Kiste, Hailey Piper, Roland Blackburn, Ira Rat, Donyae Coles, Matt Neil Hill, Brendan Vidito, LC von Hessen, Gary J. Shipley, and editors Joe Koch and Sam Richard. *Stories of the Eye* violently explores the connection of art to the body, the cosmos, madness, depression, grief, trauma, and so much more.

WEIRDPUNK STATEMENT

Made in the USA
Monee, IL
05 September 2023

42219680R00113